HAUNTED VALLEY

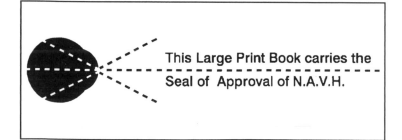

This Large Print Book carries the
Seal of Approval of N.A.V.H.

HAUNTED VALLEY

BRADFORD SCOTT

WHEELER PUBLISHING
A part of Gale, Cengage Learning

Detroit • New York • San Francisco • New Haven, Conn • Waterville, Maine • London

GALE
CENGAGE Learning˙

Copyright © 1968 by Leslie Scott.
Wheeler Publishing, a part of Gale, Cengage Learning.

LIBRARY OF CONGRESS CATALOGING-IN-PUBLICATION DATA

Scott, Bradford, 1893–1975.
    Haunted valley / by Bradford Scott.
      p. cm. — (Wheeler Publishing large print western)
    ISBN-13: 978-1-59722-805-3 (pbk. : alk. paper)
    ISBN-10: 1-59722-805-2 (pbk. : alk. paper)
      1. Large type books. I. Title.
    PS3537.C9265H38 2008
    813'.54—dc22   2008017941

Published in 2008 by arrangement with Golden West Literary Agency.

Printed in the United States of America
1 2 3 4 5 6 7 12 11 10 09 08

HAUNTED VALLEY

ONE

There are those who declare the canyon-like valley of the Canadian River is haunted. And if the spirits of murdered men can return to the scene of their death by violence, it is probably true.

For if one looks close, in the thickets, the groves, and the tangles of chaparral growth, one can see the ghostly shimmer of dry bones.

And that faint glow in the dark is not from a clump of fungus or a decaying animal. That eerie light comes from a skull.

That anguished wail that splits the curtain of the night? An owl, says the skeptic. Perhaps. But then again it could be the cry of a sinful soul in torment, doomed to wander through the eternities, alone, and never, never finding rest.

And those ruddy blotches on the stones? Just the drippings from an iron deposit. Perhaps. But it could be the noneraseable stain of blood that will lay a curse on him who touches it.

Ridiculous! But to one who believes, such fantasies are very real. And a name whispered after the sun has set may be a thing of terror indeed.

Always the Valley has known violence. The Comanches, most warlike of the Plains Tribes, rode the rough, broken through several hundred feet lower than the prairie lands north and south of it. Here the Mexican traders known as Comancheros met with them to exchange contraband goods, cattle, horses, and women and children captured from the white settlements. The Indians fought, and the Comancheros fought, and the whites who came after them fought.

Here the outlaw rode, and the widelooper, and the sheep thief. Little of peace the Valley knew.

But the Valley always attracted the humble people, who sought food and shelter in the beautiful country. The shepherd, the small farmer, the grape grower, even the raiser of a few cattle. The severe winter and spring storms gave an added attraction to the Valley because of its sheltered canyons and its broad expanses of tall grass.

Yes, always the Valley had known violence.

And now, length and breadth of the Valley, a whisper ran from mouth to mouth. A whisper and, a name. And ever the name was linked with blood and death —

"Last night *Muerto* rode again! And *Tijerna the herder — died!*"

"Just a blankety-blank outlaw who's got together a bunch of devils and is raising hell and shoving a chunk under a corner!" declared the sheriffs of Oldham, Potter and Dallam Counties, all of which had suffered from Muerto's depredations.

But the "little" people of the Valley were not so sure. A dread and sinister name, Muerto. For Muerto means "dead man"!

Can the evil dead return to work more evil? Ridiculous, of course, but not so where the ignorant and superstitious are concerned. Muerto, with his skull face, and his hand that slays! Very, very real.

Of such things, among others, Ranger Walt Slade, named by the *peones* of the Rio Grande River villages, *El Halcón* — The Hawk — was thinking as he rode Shadow, his magnificent black horse, east down the Valley, his destination Amarillo, the "Queen City of the Panhandle"-to-be, although now little more than a wild frontier town that lay something less than twenty miles south of the Valley.

As he rode, Slade hummed softly in his deep, rich voice, enjoying the beauty of the star-burned night. He wound his way through the bristles of thickets, Shadow jogging along at a steady pace.

Abruptly Slade flung up his head in an attitude of listening. From around a bend in the brush-encroached trail, no great distance ahead, had come the metallic clang of a gunshot, followed by a woman's scream vibrant with anguish and terror. Slade's voice rang cut, "Trail, Shadow, trail!"

Instantly the great horse lunged forward at racing speed, his irons pounding the trail, kicking up little spurtles of dust. Around the bend he surged, and into a little clearing where sat a lighted cabin.

Just outside the door of the cabin, outlined in a bar of light that streamed through the open door, lay the body of a man. A woman knelt beside it, wailing. And over to one side, five horsemen were methodically rounding up a small flock of sheep and getting them in marching order down the Valley.

A shout of alarm, the riders twisting in their saddles, a gleam of shifted metal, a flash of fire, and a slug fanned the weaving, ducking Ranger's face. He whipped both his big Colts from their sheaths and let drive.

The gun wielder crumpled up, pitched to the ground to lie motionless. Answering bullets whined about El Halcón. But he was shifting, slithering in the saddle, and Shadow was doing a weird, elusive dance, and none found their mark.

Another booming volley from Slade's big sixes. A second saddle was emptied. The three remaining raiders, bawling curses, spun their mounts and went crashing through the growth to the east, El Halcón streaming lead after them. He slammed his empty Colts into their sheaths, whipped his high-power Winchester from the saddle boot and sent more bullets toward the fading sound of hoofbeats. He listened a moment and his amazingly keen hearing told him the unsavory trio were not slowing. Evidently they'd had all they wanted of him for the present. He swiftly reloaded his guns, dropped to the ground and approached the man and the weeping girl who crouched beside him. She gazed up, her eyes great dark pools of terror. He flashed her a reassuring smile and knelt beside the man, who was bleeding freely from a gash in his scalp just above the hairline.

He was a rugged-looking young Mexican who very likely never had a sick day in his life. Slade found his heartbeat steady, and encouragingly strong. He probed the vicinity of the wound with sensitive fingers and could ascertain no indications of fracture. Rising, he procured a jar of antiseptic ointment and a roll of bandage from his saddle pouch.

Very quickly he had the wound smeared with the astringent ointment, heavily padded and bandaged, the flow of blood checked.

"That should hold him," he told the girl. "I don't think he's badly hurt; should be coming out of it shortly."

Again she stared at him wide-eyed, but now the expression of her dark eyes was different. She broke into speech:

"El Halcón! El Halcón, the good, the just, the compassionate, the friend of the lowly! Now I will fear no more, for now all will be well!"

Slade patted her shoulder and changed the subject.

"Know who those devils were?" he asked. She shivered.

"Muerto!" she breathed. "Muerto and his ghouls, returned from the grave, it is said, to work more evil on the living and the dead. His skull face I saw."

"No," Slade gently reproved. "Do the

spirits of the dead return, it is to right wrongs, to atone for evil done when they walked the world. So that when comes the Last Day, they can stand before the Judge with souls cleansed of sin."

"If El Halcón says it is so, it must be so," she murmured.

Slade flashed her another smile and without apparent effort picked up the heavy body of the man and carried it into the cabin, where he placed it on a nearby couch.

"Yes, he'll be okay," he told the girl. "Bullet just nicked him. See? He's regaining conciousness. Tomorrow I'll send the doctor from Amarillo to look him over, with the sheriff, who'll pick up those two bodies."

The man was indeed muttering and rolling his head from side to side. Another moment and he opened his eyes and gazed dazedly at the Ranger. Very quickly he was almost his normal self.

"Look, Rafael, look!" the girl shrilled. "It is El Halcón! Returned to earth again to right its wrongs!" She bowed her shapely head reverently, as to a shrine.

Abruptly her eyes mirrored apprehension. *Capitán,*" she said, "think you those evil ones will return?"

"I wish they would, but they won't," El Halcón replied grimly.

Rafael smiled wanly. "When one looks upon El Halcón in the hour of his wrath, one does not care to look soon again," he said. Slade smiled, and once more changed the subject.

"You are Texas born?" he asked.

"*Sí*, that is so," the other agreed.

"And Mission taught?"

"Again *Capitán* is right. Rosa, my wife, is also Texan, but not taught."

"Rafael has taught me all I need to know," Rosa interpolated cheerfully. Slade chuckled, his already-formed conclusions relative to the young couple having been confirmed.

"I think a little hot coffee would be good for him," he observed, glancing at his patient. "And I could stand a cup myself." Rosa immediately hurried to the kitchen.

"Meanwhile," Slade added, "I'll flip out the bit and loosen the cinches so my horse can graze in comfort."

Which he proceeded to do, taking time to examine the bodies of the dead outlaws by the light of the moon that was now shining brilliantly and casting its silver beams into the Valley.

After a searching glance at the contorted faces, he decided there was nothing outstanding about them. Typical Border scum, guns for hire although giving the appear-

14

ance of being above-average intelligence. Mean-looking customers, as was to be expected. He doubted that either was the notorious Muerto, because of whose recent activities Ranger Slade was in the Panhandle country. Rosa had chatted about a skull face, which very likely was a mask of vari-colored cloth. Reasonable to think that her imagination was working overtime. Which was not illogical, taking into account the stress under which she was, seeing her husband shot down before her eyes.

He did not investigate the pocket contents of the pair, preferring to leave that chore for the sheriff when he arrived. He returned to the cabin.

"And now suppose you tell me just what happened," he suggested to Rafael.

"Really, *Capitán,* there is little to tell," the Mexican replied. "When those *ladrones* rode into the clearing, I opened the door and stepped out. I saw one draw a gun, saw a blaze of light, felt pain, and then all was dark until I saw you bending over me."

While fixing coffee and a snack, Rosa took up the tale.

"When he fell as if dead, and, *nombre de dios!* I thought he was dead, they paid him no more mind, nor me," she said. "They just began rounding up the sheep."

15

"I see," Slade replied thoughtfully. "I understand sheep have been stolen from the Valley."

"That is right," said Rafael. "Many have been taken, and two herders have been killed. Were it not for *Capitán*, I think tonight would have been three."

"Possibly," Slade conceded. "I fear it is a killer bunch. I don't believe you'll be bothered any more, but I'll make sure. I have *amigos* farther down the Valley who will stand guard over your plaza for a while. Don't stray from it, and if you have a gun, don't be afraid to use it."

"I have the *escopeta*, that is known as the Sharpes, with which buffalo were slain," nodded Rafael.

"Cut loose with that old base burner and you'll blow an owlhoot clean out of the Valley," Slade answered, with a smile.

Rosa arrived with the coffee and the snack and all did full justice to her offering. After which Slade rolled a cigarette with the slim fingers of his left hand. After a few moments he got up and walked to the door, gazing out at the glow of the moonlight.

What a splendid-looking man he was, thought the young couple, and with reason.

Two

Walt Slade was very tall, more than six feet, the breadth of his shoulders and the depth of his chest commensurate with his height.

His face was arresting as his form. A rather wide mouth, grin-quirked at the corners, relieved somewhat the tinge of fierceness evinced by the prominent hawk nose above and the powerful chin and jaw beneath. Surmounting a broad forehead, his thick, crisp hair was black as Shadow's glossy midnight coat. His cheeks were lean, bronzed by sun and wind.

Slade wore with grace and distinction the homely, efficient garb of the rangeland — Levi's, the bibless overalls long favored by cowhands, soft blue shirt with vivid neckerchief looped at the throat, well scuffed half-boots of softly tanned leather, and the broad-brimmed "J.B." the rain-shed of the plains, so called by the cowboys.

Around his sinewy waist were double cartridge belts, from the carefully worked and oiled cut-out holsters of which protruded the plain black butts of heavy guns. And the observant noted that from the butts of those big Colts his slender, muscular hands seemed never far away.

Turning back to his companions, Slade

asked a question: "What's the rest of your name, Rafael?"

"Quijano," the young fellow answered.

"Quijano?" Slade repeated. "One Allende Sabida Quijano was an illustrious statesman and soldier."

"I have been told," replied Rafael, "that he was my ancestor."

"Then you have a lot to live up to," Slade said smilingly. "Try and do so, Rafael."

"*Capitán,* I will," the young fellow promised.

"And now," Slade said, "I'm heading for Amarillo."

"*Capitán,* it is a long ride, so why not spend the night with us," urged Rafael.

"Isn't very late, it's a nice night for riding, and I wish to get in touch with Sheriff Brian Carter and inform him of what happened," Slade declined. "I'll be seeing you soon, quite probably tomorrow. So *hasta luego* — till we meet again!"

"*Vaya usted con Dios* — Go you with God, *Capitán!*"

The outlaw horses, well-trained animals, had not strayed. Slade stripped off the rigs and left them to their own devices until picked up. He flipped the bit back into Shadow's mouth, tightened the cinches and mounted. Waving farewell to Quijanos, he rode east through the moonlight. He rode warily, although he doubted the outlaws would attempt something against him, not this night.

As he rode, Slade marveled at the luxuriance of the Valley growth, so markedly in contrast to the flat, almost treeless prairie above, an oasis in a "desert" of grass. There were stands of big wild plums, wild choke berries, gooseberries, grapes, flowering shrubs in profusion, wide stretches of tall grass. Once rid of the pest of outlawry, it might well be a garden to rival Eden.

Living water sang its sprightly song and chuckled to itself over outlandish and doubtless ribald secrets of its own. The brush rustled to the movements of little animals cheerfully going about their various businesses, and now and then a night bird called, the very voice of the wastelands bidding one welcome and farewell.

There were ways to enter or leave the Valley with its precipitous sides and walls of rock. Many were known to but few, and the majority were difficult to negotiate. An exception was the great crossing at Tascosa, where several creeks converged on the north side of the river and there were broad meadows of spring-fed grass. Here for ages the buffalo and other wild animals crossed to the south plains, pausing to feed on the tall grass. The Indians and the white explorers followed their trails.

Walt Slade knew of a little known descent into the Valley which was so hidden by straggles of brush and tall grass as to be almost indiscernible from only a few yards distant, either at the crest of the wall or at its base.

With his unerring instinct for distance and direction, after covering a few miles down the Valley and then a couple more to the south, he located the zig-zag that passed for a trail, which Shadow, with a few snorts of disgust, negotiated without difficulty. And but a short distance from the lip of the great trough was a fairly well-traveled trail that led to Amarillo.

With a searching glance that took in the moon-drenched prairie in every direction and found it deserted, he turned into the trail and continued on his way at a brisk pace.

The miles flowed back, the minutes grew to hours, and finally he saw a sparkle of lights, like fallen stars, that marked the site of Amarillo, the new "Cowboy Capital" of the plains, the title inherited from dying Tascosa in the Canadian Valley.

In the beginning Amarillo had boasted the

elegant soubriquet of "Ragtown" when it was but a collection of buffalo-hide huts sprawled beside the railroad tracks and serving as a supply depot and shipping point for the buffalo hunters then sweeping the last of the great herds from the prairies.

But when Slade sighted the town that night, there were already plenty of substantial buildings and more being erected, although quite a few of the hide huts clung tenaciously to existence.

Half an hour later found him riding through the outskirts of the pueblo by way of Filmore Street.

Late though it was, there were plenty of people on the streets and in the saloons and other places of entertainment.

With his first thought to his horse, he paused at a small stable where Shadow had been domiciled before. Knocking on the door roused the old keeper, who appeared with a cocked-sawed-off shotgun in his hand. He remembered Slade and his mount and had a warm greeting for both. On a previous occasion, he had been duly introduced to Shadow, a one-man horse who allowed nobody to put a hand on him without his master's sanction, and the big black permitted himself to be led to a stall and a generous helping of oats, while the

21

keeper at once got busy with currycomb and brush.

"Have him shining when you come for him," he assured El Halcón.

Knowing that Shadow would receive the best of care, and that his rig and rifle were in safe hands, Slade shouldered his pouches and repaired to a hotel on Tyler Street he had patronized before and registered for a room, in which he stored his pouches.

He did not visit the sheriff's office, for at such a late hour, Sheriff Carter wouldn't be likely to be there. Slade had a good notion as to where the old peace officer would be located and made his way to Swivel-eye Sanders' big Trail End saloon and restaurant.

It quickly developed that he guessed right. Seated at a table with a hefty snort of red-eye in front of him was big, bulky, and rugged-faced Sheriff Carter.

"So! Made it, eh?" he chuckled as they shook hands. "Had a hunch you would today, that's why I stayed up, sorta waiting on you. But you're mighty late. Something hold you up?"

"Sort of, for a while," Slade answered.

The sheriff looked expectant, so Slade recounted his experience with the sheep thieves and the Quijanos. Carter listened intently, and made several blasphemous remarks.

"Muerto, all right, not much doubt as to that," he said when the Ranger paused. "He's vicious as a teased sidewinder, and so are the blasted wind spiders that ride with him."

"How did he collect that bizarre name?" Slade asked.

"Darned if I know for sure," Carter replied. "Maybe he put it out himself, or maybe some terrapin-brain tied it onto him. Sounds plumb loco."

"To us, yes," Slade said soberly. "But not to the ignorant and superstitious, of which, unfortunately, there are quite a few in the Valley and elsewhere in the section. To them, such a notion as an evil spirit rising from the grave is unpleasantly real. They actually believe such a thing can happen, and so numb with fright as a consequence." He paused to roll and light a cigarette and then resumed, reminiscently:

"Down in the Rio Grande River country, a while back, there was a bunch of hellions that pretended to be the reincarnation of the 'Iron Men of Spain,' who invaded and conquered the country centuries before. The head of the outfit operated a small canning factory and went so far as to fashion a fair simulacrum of ancient armor from sheets of tin. Looked to be the real thing, but wouldn't stop a forty-five slug.

"The *peons* of the river villages and others of similar ilk were scared blue. To such an extent that they wouldn't talk to law enforcement officers, or anybody else, for that matter. No matter what depredations were committed against them and others, they refused to loosen the latigos on their jaws, which of course worked to the advantage of the outlaws."

"But I've a notion they did a mite of talking after El Halcón showed up," interpolated the sheriff. "Right?"

"Yes, they did talk some then," Slade admitted smilingly.

"What become of the outlaws?" Carter asked.

"They died," was the laconic response.

THREE

The sheriff shook with laughter. "Plumb usual El Halcón ending," he chuckled. "And you figure we're up against something like that here?"

"Looks a little that way," Slade conceded. "It would appear your *amigo* Muerto is an unusually competent individual, in more ways than one, and able to impress people with his nonsense. I would not classify Rosa Quijano as of the ignorant and superstitious type, but although I don't think she really believes the yarn, there is no doubt but it had a disquieting effect on her. Rafael, no. Well, we'll see. Now suppose you give me the lowdown on what's been happening here that's got you worked up. I've been down in the corner of the State and am rather out of touch with conditions here."

"There's been plenty happening, of the wrong sort, the past couple of months," Carter growled. "That's why I wrote McNelty asking for help, and to send you along if you happened to be around. He wired me you were on your way."

"Funny how things work out," Slade interrupted. "I took the train to Channing then, being to the north and west of Amarillo, all of a sudden decided to ride the Valley the rest of the way; I always liked the Valley, especially on a bright and sunny day. Otherwise, I wouldn't have happened along when Muerto and his horned toads were at work. Go ahead with what you have to tell me."

"Nothing good," said Carter. "Tascosa stage robbed of nigh onto ten thousand dollars, driver shot. Hurt pretty bad, but Doc Beard pulled him through. Three saloons robbed right here in town. A lot of sheep stole outa the Valley. Same goes for wide-looped cows from the spreads on both sides of the river. A general store burgled. They've been having it even worse up in Dallam County, especially where widelooped cows are concerned. Ranchers up there are going broke."

"With the Oklahoma hills handy, Dallam is particularly vulnerable to rustling," Slade interjected. "Begins to look a little like the good old days of Veck Sosna and his Co-mancheros."

"Worse," snorted the sheriff. "With Sosna, you at least knew who to look for. Just the opposite with Muerto. He's a ghost, all right, so far as anybody dropping a loop on who the devil he is. That is, if he ain't the Devil himself, which I'm almost inclined to believe."

"No idea at all who he might be, then?"

"Just about the size of it," replied Carter. "I've got my eye on a hellion or two, of course, but none of 'em seem to exactly qualify. He's a blasted shadow, comes and goes like a breath of wind packing a bad smell."

"Sounds like an ambitious and interesting gent," Slade commented. "Will be a pleasure to try conclusions with him."

26

"You and your notions of pleasure!" snorted the sheriff. "And don't forget, after what you did in the Valley tonight, you're a marked man to Muerto. He'll very likely come looking for you."

"Might work to our advantage," Slade replied cheerfully. "Seeing as we have no idea where to look for *him.*" The sheriff gave vent to another disgusted snort and beckoned a waiter.

"Feel in the notion of a bite to eat to hold the likker down," he said. "What you going to have?"

"Had a snack with the Quijanos, but that was quite a while ago, so I think I can put away another one and some coffee," Slade admitted.

They gave their order to the waiter, and at that moment the door to the back room opened and big, burly and bony Swivel-eye Sanders, the owner, appeared. He came plowing across the room with his rolling, sailor-like gait, hand outstretched, and boomed a welcome to Slade.

Swivel-eye came honestly by his peculiar nickname. His eyes did seem to swivel in every direction. One eyelid hung continually lower than the other and viewed from a certain angle lent his otherwise rather saturnine face an air of droll and unexpected

27

waggery; he seemed to glower with one eye and leer jocosely with the other. One profile appeared jovial, the other sinister. A sudden full-face and the viewer was bewildered and didn't know just what conclusion to arrive at.

But he was a square-shooter and ran his big and prosperous place strictly on the up-and-up; nobody need fear being mistreated or taken advantage of in the Trail End.

After shaking hands with Slade, Swivel-eye hustled to the kitchen to tell the cook to rattle his hocks with something special, which the old Mexican culinary artist proceeded to do.

"Sure fine to have you with us again, Mr. Slade," said Swivel-eye, when he returned from the kitchen. "Now we'll get some results, eh, Sheriff?"

"Done got some already," Carter returned cheerfully and regaled Sanders with a somewhat colored account of Slade's brush with the outlaws in the Canadian River Valley. Swivel-eye did not appear in the least surprised.

"Yep, business is due to pick up," said Swivel. "Have a snort, Mr. Slade, have another, Sheriff. Everything on the house, of course. Won't have it otherwise. This is a day to celebrate. Waiter!"

"After we finish eating, I'm going to knock off a few hours of shuteye," Slade said. "About midmorning we'll head for the Valley to pick up the bodies and see how the Quijanos are making out."

"Fine!" replied the sheriff. "You can show us an easy way to get down in that blasted gulch, and where the carcasses are. I'll send word to Doc Beard, in case he figures he should go along for a look at Rafael's head. Expect he will, but he'll take your word for it that there ain't likely to be any complications. One of my deputies is out of town right now, but I reckon with the one that's here we should make out."

"No reason why we shouldn't," Slade agreed.

After putting away a really excellent repast, Slade went back to the kitchen to thank the cook and his helpers, and left them beaming. Reaching his hotel room without incident, he tumbled into bed and was almost instantly asleep.

When Slade awoke, sunlight was shining brightly through chinks in the blind. He bathed, shaved, donned a clean shirt and overalls and headed for the Trail End and some breakfast, where he found Sheriff Carter, Ed Grumley, the deputy, and old Doc Beard assembled.

"Doubt if I'll be needed, after you took care of things," he said to Slade. "But it's a nice day for a ride and I've been cooped up of late — business is mighty good in this hell town. So I figure to mosey along with you work dodgers. Might be able to do a little business on the way."

Slade chuckled as Doc swung back his coat to reveal a long-barreled old forty-four. If he got the chance, Doc would very likely "make" some business; he was a salty old gent.

"I tied onto a couple of pack mules — they're at the stable — and we'll be all set to go as soon as you finish your surrounding," Carter said.

Half an hour later found them jogging across the sun-drenched prairie under a sky of real Texas blue. Slade thoroughly enjoyed the ride, but as they drew near the brush-fringed lip of the Valley, he became very much on the alert, constantly studying the growth with eyes that missed nothing.

However, he detected no signs of movement in the chaparral, and birds fluttering over the thickets showed no signs of alarm. Just the same, he breathed relief when they finally reached the growth without incident. Out on the prairie they would have been settin' quail for fair, were a few drygulchers

30

holed up in the brush and he had failed to spot them. He had thought it unlikely, but from a rapscallion of Muerto's reputation, anything could be expected.

"So here it is," remarked Carter, "your own private back door to that blasted gulch; I'd never have noticed it. Guess there ain't anything those telescopic eyes of yours don't see."

Without trouble, they negotiated the not too difficult descent to the Valley floor and rode west along the river bank, where a semblance of a trail ran. Slade constantly surveyed the growth ahead, his ears mostly slanted toward the river, which he also studied, for the stream was low, its flow placid, and sound travels well over still water.

It was his amazingly keen eyesight that saved them from disaster. Abruptly he snapped, in low tones, "Hold it!"

FOUR

The posse jolted to a halt, glancing at him inquiringly.

"What is it?" Carter asked, instinctively keeping his voice down.

Slade gestured to the river, where a small white cylinder was drifting slowly down stream on the surface. Even as they gazed, it disintegrated to a slip of waterlogged paper and, to El Halcón's eyes, at least, a sprinkling of tiny brown particles that instantly sank.

"What the devil was it?" Carter repeated.

"A half-smoked cigarette," Slade replied in little above a whisper. "It was tossed in the water a little the other side of that bend ahead, and close. Otherwise the paper would have shredded out and spilled the tobacco before it reached here. Sombody in the brush around that bend. May mean nothing, but we're not taking any chances. Unfork and shove the horses and the mules into the growth, and hope they'll keep quiet."

Quickly and without question, the maneuver was accomplished. Slade felt pretty sure the docile animals would remain still. As to Shadow he had no qualms. He just dropped the split reins to the ground, knowing the big black would remain motionless until he returned.

"Now follow behind me, step where I step, and for Pete's sake don't make a noise," El Halcón cautioned. With which he began worming his way through the brush, the others following. Often he paused to peer and listen.

They reached the brush-grown bend, eased around it. Slade called a halt; to his straining ears had come a sound, a low mutter of voices. Now there was no doubt in his mind that concealed in the brush directly ahead were the drygulchers, all set to mow down the posse as, following the trail, they rounded the bend.

Slade experienced a surge of hot anger. They would be justified in shooting the murderous devils without warning. But they were law enforcement officers and must conduct themselves as such. He eased forward a couple more steps, the others crowding beside him, and they saw the shadowy form of the outlaws, lounging easily at the outer fringe of the brush that edged the trail, their eyes fixed on the bend, waiting for the appearance of their unsuspecting victims. Glints of metal showed they held guns in their hands.

"You do the talking, Brian," Slade breathed to the sheriff. "Must give them a chance to surrender. They won't take it, so shoot fast, and shoot straight. Now!"

The sheriff's voice rang out, shattering the silence —

"Up! In the name of the law!"

A chorus of startled exclamations, a wheeling to face the sound, and a jutting forward of guns.

"Let them have it!" Slade roared, and shot with both hands. Answering slugs whipped leaves and twigs from the growth. It was poor shooting light, but a drygulcher fell before the first thundering volley. Slade squeezed trigger again and saw a man hurtled sideways to the ground. He also got a flickering glimpse of a form dashing into the brush, snapped a shot at it but knew he did not score. Beside him sounded the sullen boom of Doc Beard's old "persuader," and the remaining owlhoot went down. Slade dashed forward, but slowed as he heard a beat of hoofs fading away upstream. One of the devils had escaped. No sense in trying to run him down, even could he retrieve his horse in time. The fugitive, doubtless thoroughly familiar with the Valley, could turn off anywhere, or could hole up and wait for his pursuer, the advantage all with him. Slade turned to his companions.

"Anybody hurt?" he asked anxiously.

Sheriff Carter was swabbing the blood that trickled from a bullet burn along his cheek. Grumley, the deputy, had been slightly nicked in the left hand. Slade and Beard were untouched.

"Figured I'd do some business this trip,"

34

Doc said cheerfully. "Wait till I fetch my satchel."

Carter was chortling over the bodies of the slain outlaws.

"Fine!" he said. "Three out of four. Not bad at all."

"But could have been better, for I'm greatly of the opinion that the one who escaped was Muerto himself," Slade replied. "A regular hairtrigger brain he has. Took advantage of the confusion and hightailed."

"Get a look at him?" asked Carter.

"Not at his face," Slade regretted. "It was in the shadow when he turned. Looked to be rather tall and big, but couldn't say for sure in this dim light. The foliage above is a veritable mat the sunbeams can't penetrate."

"Mean-looking cusses, these three, wouldn't you say?" the sheriff remarked.

"About average, perhaps appearing more intelligent than most," was Slade's verdict. "Let's see what they have on them."

The drygulchers' pockets divulged nothing Slade considered of significance save a surprisingly large sum of money, which the sheriff packed away.

"Hellions have been doing pretty well by themselves," he commented. "County treasury's getting rich. Always does when you're around, Walt."

A search failed to locate the horses ridden by the slain outlaws. Evidently, frightened by the gun battle, they had followed the one ridden by the escaper.

"Somebody in the Valley will quickly pick them up, so they won't suffer," Slade said. "Anyway, we haven't time to go looking for them."

"Guess we'll hafta tie onto some more mules and come back tomorrow to fetch these carcasses in," decided Carter. "You'll have quite a collection to hold an inquest on, Doc."

"Just a waste of time, but the law's the law," grunted Doc, who was coroner.

The outlaws' guns, good arms, were collected and stowed in a saddle pouch, the trifling injuries suffered by Carter and Grumley cared for, and the posse resumed its interrupted ride up the Valley, Slade keeping a sharp lookout. Didn't seem logical that Muerto would chance holding up to risk a shot at them, but he already had proven himself a master of the unexpected and El Halcón was taking no chances.

Finally the Quijano cabin came into view, and Slade abruptly exclaimed, "Hold it! Somebody besides the Quijanos in that shack."

However, another moment and his fears

36

were allayed as three dark-faced young men, rifles under their arms, stepped out the door, Rafael Quijano following. All bowed low to El Halcón.

"News travels fast in the Valley," Rafael explained. "When the *amigos* heard of what happened, and what *Capitán* desired, they came at once."

"Nice of them," Slade replied, voicing a greeting in flawless Spanish that caused them to smile with pleasure.

Rafael gestured to a small corral back of the cabin, in which were the two outlaw horses Slade had loosed the night before, with a couple of complacent looking mules keeping them company.

"Them we caught and saved for *Capitán*," he said.

"Fine!" chuckled Carter. "One more critter and we'll be all set to pack in the whole passel of carcasses."

"You are welcome to the loan of one of my mules," Rafael said.

"Much obliged, that'll help," the sheriff accepted. With Slade lending a hand, he gave the two bodies in the clearing a once-over, again discovering a hefty passel of *dinero*. He glanced at Slade, who nodded, and divided the money into two portions, one of which he handed to the three young Mexicans who were standing guard over the Quijanos, the other to Rafael.

"You'll need some to pay the doctor's bill," he remarked.

"Nope, no bill," said Beard. "This ain't a professional trip; today I'm just one of the boys."

However, he examined Rafael's wound and applied a fresh bandage.

"Leave it on over tomorrow and then take it off and forget it," he directed. "Just a nick. But had it been an inch to the right, you'd have been a goner."

"And were it not for *Capitán,* I quite likely would have been anyway," said Rafael.

"Uh-huh, wouldn't put it past the sidewinders to have plugged you again when they saw you weren't dead," growled the sheriff. "Well, five of them won't do any more pluggin' in this world. Right now, they're handlin' coal shovels instead of guns."

"*El Dios* is good, in the fires of *infierno* doubtless they burn," one of the young Mexicans interpolated piously. "If there's any justice, and I figure there is," agreed Carter.

Rosa called them to coffee and a bountiful snack. After which the bodies of the

38

outlaws were loaded onto the horses they had ridden in life and the posse headed for town, pausing to secure the three bodies beside the river.

Progress with the led animals was slow and it was nearing midnight when they reached Amarillo. However, the streets were still crowded with merrymakers and others, and they acquired quite an entourage on their way to the sheriff's office, where the bodies were laid out for inspection.

Wrangles arose as to whether or not the outlaws had been seen in town. Slade listened, but learned nothing he considered significant.

"May have better luck when some night bartenders show up tomorrow for a look, barkeeps see everything," said the sheriff. "Well, guess there's nothing more to do here."

Pretty well worn out by the long and turbulent day, everybody went to bed.

When Slade awoke, around midmorning, he did not at once descend to breakfast. Instead, he sat by the open window, gazing out at the sun glow, and thinking.

Well, at least he had made a start. Not too bad, considering the length of time he had been in the section. However, he was not at all complacent about the situation as it stood. He was inclined to believe with the sheriff, that he was up against something that might well tax the abilities of El Halcón. The individual who called himself Muerto was without doubt a brilliant and capable man who had for some reason or other taken the wrong fork in the trail. Something akin to the late unlamented Veck Sosna, who could have written both M.D. and Ph.D. after his name, had he chosen to do so. Probably more dangerous even than the leader of the Comancheros, whose overweening conceit was a weakness.

Well, he or one of his followers had made the sort of slip the outlaw band seemed always prone to make, by tossing the cigarette butt into the river instead of pinching it out and dropping it to the ground. A little thing, seemingly a mere trifle, but the salvation of the posse, including himself, who very likely would have been the prime target. Maybe the gentleman would be considerate enough to make another of some sort. Not to be relied on, however.

What he did rely on was a stiffening of the courage of the Valley dwellers once they learned that El Halcón was present and assuring them that Muerto was no evil spirit risen from the grave but just another bad man with the forked end down and a hat on top.

The rough and hardy shepherds and herders might shake with terror at the shadows in their own minds, but they would not fear a mortal foe no matter how ruthless and resourceful. They would begin to talk. Every move made by Muerto would be noted and reported to him, which would afford him an advantage over the outlaw leader not enjoyed by local law enforcement officers.

Not that Muerto was to be taken lightly. Far from it. There was little doubt in Slade's mind but that he was an evil genius of a high order and must be dealt with accordingly. Well, he'd gone up against that sort before and had always made out. And he had to admit that, reprehensible though it might be, he would get a certain enjoyment from pitting his guns and his wits against such a character. He headed for the Trail End and breakfast in an equable frame of mind.

FIVE

Although the hour was early, the Trail End was already quite busy. As he gave his order, Slade noted Swivel-eye at the far end of the bar talking with a tall, well-formed man whose deeply bronzed complexion evidenced much experience with sun and weather. His features were regular, his mouth firm to tightness, his hair dark. Slade believed his eyes were light blue, the distance being too great to be sure.

As Slade sat down and gave his order, Swivel-eye waved to him. A moment later he and his compaion crossed the room to Slade's table.

"Mr. Slade," Sanders said. "I want you to know Mr. Watson Gaynard. Mr. Gaynard, this is Mr. Walt Slade, Sheriff Carter's special deputy we were talking about."

"It's a pleasure to know you, Mr. Slade," said Gaynard, his voice deep and resonant. He extended a big hand. His grip was powerful, but not particularly impressive to El Halcón, whose slender fingers could crack a new horseshoe.

"Have a chair and join me in breakfast," Slade said.

"I've already eaten, but I'll join you in a drink," Gaynard accepted as he sat down. Swivel-eye also occupied a chair.

"Mr. Gaynard is in the drilling business," he announced. "Expects to put down a well hereabouts if things work out right."

"Oil, Mr. Gaynard?" Slade asked. The other shook his head, smilingly.

42

"No, Mr. Slade, water," he replied. "The way this town is growing, it is but a matter of time, and a short time at that, when more water than is now available will be badly needed. The lake water is not fit for human consumption, and the windmills, tanks and shallow wells will not be able to supply the want. I am trying to interest the Amarillo businessmen in the project. Deep wells tapping the reservoir I am confident exists far underground will be absolutely essential and they alone will solve the problem."

"Sounds reasonable," Slade admitted.

"It is reasonable," Gaynard declared vigorously. "I have made a study of such matters and know whereof I speak. Soon I intend to sink a test well and will prove my point, after I have decided on a suitable spot on the prairie near town. Hope you'll see fit to visit the project once it gets started. I'll be only too glad to explain the rather intricate details."

Swivel-eye, who was fairly familiar with Slade's background, stifled a grin. However, he offered no comment.

"Thank you, Mr. Gaynard," Slade replied. "Chances are I will."

"I feel sure you'll find it interesting," Gaynard said. "I figure that before long twenty or even twenty-five wells will be needed.

I'm trying to talk it up to the business people. Have an appointment with several this morning, so I'll have to be moving along. Thanks for the drink, and you must allow me to reciprocate next time, which I hope will be soon." With a smile and a nod, he departed.

"Well, what do you think?" Swivel asked as the swinging doors closed on Gaynard's broad back.

"That he is absolutely right," Slade replied. "Sooner than most folks realize, the lack of water is going to pose a problem for Amarillo. His estimate as to the number of deep wells that will be required is conservative. Forty will eventually be more like it."

(Slade's prediction would be proven remarkably correct.)

"It will be a costly project, what with pumping facilities and piping," the Ranger continued. "But it is inevitable and the people might as well face up to the facts. Gaynard may have trouble convincing the business people that the need is urgent, but if he fails and the project is put off, the ultimate expense will be much greater. They would do well to cooperate with him, if he is proven capable."

"Seems to know his business, all right," Swivel commented. "Showed up a couple of months back, didn't say what his business was. Spent a lot of time riding around over the prairie. Would stop and look at a place, then ride on and look at another."

"Resolving on a suitable spot for his test well, I imagine," Slade remarked.

"Guess so," agreed Swivel. "Got in touch with the bank president and put his cards on the table. Business has been argued ever since. Some for it, some against it, saying there is no hurry."

"They'll end up realizing their mistake," Slade predicted, a trifle grimly.

"I predict, too," he added, "that sooner or later the city will buy a section of land down to the southwest in the shallow water belt and drill there also, and pipe the water to town."

(Which also proved to be the case.)

"Well, if you say it's so, Mr. Slade, I reckon it is so, seein' as folks who know say you're one of the best engineers in Texas."

"I fear they tend to exaggerate," Slade answered smilingly.

"Got a notion folks like Coddington, the big railroad man up at Delhart, Jim Hogg, who used to be governor, 'Bet a Million' Gates of Wall Street, and old Jim Dunn who runs the whole C. & P. Railroad System ain't given to talking just to hear their heads rattle," Swivel differed. "Me, I'll string along with 'em."

Swivel-eye wasn't too far from the truth. Shortly before the death of his father, which followed financial difficulties that entailed the loss of the elder Slade's ranch, young Walt had graduated with high honors from a noted college of engineering. He had planned to take a postgraduate course to round out his education. That, however, became out of the question for the time being and when Captain Jim McNelty, with whom Walt had worked some during summer vacations, suggested he sign up with the Rangers for a while and pursue his studies in spare time, Slade fell in with the idea and became a Texas Ranger.

Long since he had gotten more from private study than he could have hoped for from the postgrad and had received attractive offers of employment from big men of the business and financial world he had contacted in the course of his Ranger activities.

But Ranger work had gotten a strong hold on him, as shrewd old Captain Jim doubtless figured it would, offering as it did so many opportunities for righting wrongs, curbing evil, helping the deserving, and making Texas a better land for the right kind of people. He was loath to sever connections with the illustrious band of law enforcement officers. He was young, plenty of time to become an engineer, later; he'd stick with the Rangers for a while.

Slade found Mr. Gaynard's plans, problems and activities of interest, but they did not tend to further the solution of his own problem, so far as he could see, the problem of running down the elusive Muerto and putting a stop to *his* plans and activities.

So he put the driller out of his mind and addressed himself to his delayed breakfast with the appetite of youth and perfect digestion.

"You've sure got folks jabberin' over what happened yesterday and night before last, Mr. Slade," Swivel-eye chuckled. "Some wanted to talk to you about it, but I told 'em to leave you alone till you finished your meal."

"Thanks," Slade replied gratefully. "I'm glad of the chance to eat in peace. Has the sheriff been in yet?"

"Not yet," Swivel answered. "Expect him any minute. He was at the office a little while ago, with some night bartenders who were having a look at those carcasses you packed in."

He glanced around, lowered his voice. "I ain't plum sure, but I think a couple of those sidewinders were in here a few nights back, just before the Tascosa stage was held up and robbed. I'd say the bunch of 'em hang around in town a good deal. With all the comings and goings here, nobody would pay them any attention so long as they behaved themselves."

With which Slade agreed. There was a constant stream of transients through Amarillo. Some who lingered for a while, others who just stopped over for a day.

Swivel-eye was tugging his mustache, his brow wrinkling. He shook his head and growled.

"I'm gettin' surer by the minute that those two rapscallions were here," he declared in a complaining voice. "And it seems to me they were talking with somebody I oughta remember, but can't, though I'm tryin' to."

"Keep on trying," Slade advised. "Might mean something, never can tell."

"I will," Swivel promised. "Let you know right away if it comes to me. Here's the sheriff. Maybe he'll have something to tell you."

The sheriff didn't have much. "Yep, a coupla barkeeps are pretty sure they served one or another of those hellions, but don't remember anything partickler about 'em," he said. "Usually the way. Jiggers musta left good tips. Otherwise the drink jugglers woulda kept 'em in mind against the next time. Not leaving a barkeep a tip is almost as dangerous as to forget payin' a rumhole keeper for a drink."

"Some folks I could mention have mighty bad memories," Swivel-eye remarked pointedly. "Have a snort, Sheriff, on the house. Then you won't have to strain your forgettery."

Slade managed to finish his breakfast without further interruption. Over a final cup of steaming coffee, he studied the already crowded room, spotting several questionable-looking characters. However, he had learned from experience not to put too much dependence on outward appearances. He knew well there is no such thing as a criminal physiognomy. The exterior of a saint may well overlay the character of a devil, and vice versa. The face of an Abbe Maury like the seven cardinal sins may be but the result of physically ill-mated ancestry.

For the sheriff's benefit, Slade recounted Swivel-eye's suspicions anent the two slain outlaws. Carter listened with interest.

"Here's hoping the jigger gets his think

49

tank working and does remember who the sidewinders were bagging with," he said when the Ranger paused. "Might do us some good."

"Yes, it might provide the lead we are sorely in need of," Slade agreed. "Right now we haven't the slightest notion which way to turn, who Muerto is or who is lined up behind him. I have hopes that the Valley dwellers may come up with something, now they are not afraid to talk. They have sharp eyes and might well spot something worthwhile. Well, we'll see."

"Yep, guess your El Halcón reputation is paying off, per usual, but, blast it! That El Halcón business bothers me. I'm always scairt some mistaken deputy or marshal may plug you sometime, having you at a disadvantage, because you wouldn't want to kill a peace officer. Or some professional gun slinger hankerin' to be known as the downer of the fastest gunhand in the whole Southwest might take a shot at your back."

"I'll risk it," Slade replied carelessly.

"Oh, I know," snorted Carter. "Chances are the marshal would just lose his iron and a chunk of his hand, and the gun slinger wouldn't be bothering the community any more, but just the same it bothers me."

Owing to his habit of working under cover

as much as possible and often not revealing his Ranger connections, Walt Slade had built up a peculiar double reputation. Those, like Sheriff Carter, who knew the truth were wont to declare he was not only the most fearless but the ablest of the Rangers. Others, who knew him only as El Halcón with killings to his credit, insisted he was just an outlaw himself, too smart to get caught, so far. Still others who knew him as El Halcón were his stanch defenders, maintaining that he always fought on the side of law and order with peace officers of unblemished repute, and that anybody he killed had a killing coming.

And the *peones* and other humble people said, "El Halcón! The just, the good, the compassionate, the friend of the lowly! May *El Dios* ever guard him!" Which Slade valued above all else.

The deception also worried Captain Jim McNelty, the famed Commander of the Border Battalion of the Texas Rangers, who, like Sheriff Carter, feared his Lieutenant and ace-man might come to harm because of it.

But Slade would point out that as El Halcón, avenues of information were opened to him that would be closed to a known Ranger, and that outlaws, thinking him one of their own brand, sometimes got careless, very much to their sorrow.

So Captain Jim did not forbid the deception and Slade went his careless way as El Halcón and bothered about possible consequences not at all.

SIX

"Well, shall we amble over to the office and see if anything has turned up?"

"Not a bad idea," Slade agreed, and started to rise.

"Hold it a minute!" Carter exclaimed. "See the feller who just came in?" Slade did.

The newcomer was tall and broad. He had an impassive, leathery face, prominent features, a tight mouth, and hard, watchful dark eyes. His hair also was dark, and slightly sprinkled with gray.

"What about him?" Slade asked.

"Name's Meader, Jeff Meader," the sheriff replied. "Showed up here about three months back. Bought the old Fitch place to the north of the part of John Fletcher's and Keith Norman's holdings that are on the north side of the river. You'll remember it, narrow north by south but long east by west. Runs clean across Oldham County to the New Mexico line."

The sheriff paused, watching Meader make his way to the bar not far from where Swivel-eye Sanders was standing.

"Well?" Slade prompted.

"Remember me sayin' I had my eye on a hellion or two?" said Carter. "He's one of 'em."

"Why?" Slade asked.

"Well, for one thing, he's a plumb salty hellion and has a salty bunch riding for him. Wants to be left alone and lets everybody know it. Has been in two or three ruckuses in the rumholes down at the south end of town. Sorta wrecked one place, but I gather he didn't start it. And it was mighty soon after he landed here that things began happening, especially cow and sheep stealing, and you know it's a straight shoot across his holding to the New Mexico hills, where the buyers of widelooped critters hang out."

"Anything more than suspicion to go on?" Slade asked.

"Reckon not," the sheriff was forced to admit.

"Then it's best to be chary of insinuating," Slade said. "You could be doing the man a grave injustice."

"Oh, I haven't mentioned to anybody 'cept you," Carter replied. "I'm just thinking."

"Okay, so long as you don't think out loud," Slade said, smilingly.

He studied Jeff Meader for a moment, and held his judgment in abeyance until he had learned more about the gentleman.

"Shall we make another try for the office?" Carter suggested.

Slade was agreeable and they set out. El Halcón noticed that Meader, talking with Swivel-eye, followed their progress to the door with his eyes.

They found everything quiet at the office, Deputy Grumley, his hand bandaged, smoking the pipe of peace. He had nothing to report.

Later in the afternoon, Doc Beard, the coroner, held an inquest on the five slain owlhoots. The jury's verdict justified their killing and expressed a hope that soon there would be another inquest on more of the same brand. The jurors received their pay and hurried to the Trail End to get rid of it as quickly as possible.

"And now what?" Carter asked.

"I think I'll take a walk around town and over to the railroad yards, which I see have been expanded some more since I was here."

"Yep, business is sure picking up," agreed the sheriff. "At this rate, we're going to end up with a real town. That is, if we can get rid of the infernal owlhoots that will scare folks away, and maybe cause some who are already here to move. Oh, well, with El Halcón on the job, I reckon it's just a matter of time. Five a day ain't at all bad."

"If we can count on enough of that sort of days," Slade said, falling in with the sheriff's humor.

"I'm betting on it," declared Deputy Grumley. "How about some coffee 'fore you mosey? Got a pot simmerin' on the back room stove."

"Best thing you've said yet," Slade accepted.

While they were drinking the coffee, a couple more night bartenders dropped in for a look, with them several men in cowhand garb, whose faces were not familiar to Slade.

The blankets were removed. The barkeeps took a look and shook their heads. But one of those accompanying them, a middle-sized, alert-appearing individual, peered close and uttered an exclamation.

"I saw that chunky one four days back," he said. "Remember him because of that knife scar across his cheek."

"Where'd you see him?" the sheriff asked.

"Up to the north of the Tascosa crossing,"

the informant replied. "I was heading for Tascosa and I reckon they were coming from there."

"How far to the north?"

"Oh, maybe fifteen miles. Don't know whose holding I was riding over — haven't been here for quite a while and have sorta lost track of folks. I did notice some cows wearin' a Triangle M brand, don't remember seein' that burn when I was here before."

Carter shot Slade a significant glance, but the Ranger refrained from comment.

"Remember anything about the hellion?" the sheriff pursued. The cowhand, or at least he appeared to be one, shook his head.

"There was another jigger ridin' with him," he explained. "They 'peared to be giving me a mighty close once-over, and I didn't like their looks, so I kept right on ridin'; glad to see the last of them."

The sheriff nodded, and looked pleased. Slade decided he preferred not to discuss the matter until he had time to think it over and shoved his empty cup aside and stood up to go.

"Heading for any place in particular, Walt?" Carter asked.

"Oh, chances are I'll amble down to the southwest edge of town and watch the sunset," El Halcón replied. "May drop in at the Washout for a gab with Thankful Yates, the owner. Then as I said, I'll head for the railroad yards. Want to have a look at the new gravity hump they've put in since I was here last."

"Uh-huh, and maybe they'll need you to straighten out that one, like you did that other one when you were here," said Carter. "Okay, I'll meet you at the Trail End for a surrounding."

As he walked slowly down town Slade mulled over what the chuckline rider, for as such El Halcón catalogued him, had to say. Carter was evidently convinced that it helped to build a case against Jeff Meader, the Triangle M owner, but Slade felt it was of dubious significance. The fact that the two outlaws were riding across Meader's land was no proof that Meader was associated with them. The old peace officer was "set in his ways" as the saying went, and once he became suspicious of somebody, it was difficult to get him to change his mind.

Not that Slade definitely discarded the bit of information. Under the circumstances, anything that appeared to bear on the Muerto problem must be given consideration. So he stored it in the back of his mind for possible future reference and for the time being forgot all about it. Later, the true significance of the incident would be glaringly apparent.

At a leisurely gait, he worked his way toward the south-western edge of the pueblo, studying the faces of passersby, listening to snatches of conversation. He paused briefly at a couple of places, but contacted nothing he considered of interest. Finally, he leaned against a convenient lamppost and watched the sunset flame its many-colored splendor, until the vivid hues faded, the sky turned from deepest blue to steely gray, then black, with the stars blossoming in gold-flecked silver.

A little later, he entered the Washout, a saloon and restaurant almost as large as the Trail End and excellently appointed.

Thankful Yates, the owner, big, burly, fiercely mustached, hurried to greet him warmly.

"Plumb fine to see you back, Mr. Slade," he said. "Wait till I tie onto a bottle of my private stock. We'll have a couple together and you can tell me what you've been doing with yourself. Understand you've been sorta busy since you landed here. Fine! Fine! Keep up the good work; we can stand a lot of it."

They sat and chatted for a while, then

58

Slade departed, promising Yates he'd see him again soon.

He would, sooner than he expected.

After leaving the Washout, Slade headed for the railroad yards and the gravity hump he wished to inspect. He entered the yards about midway from the hump at the upper end and started walking in that direction, following the lead that would eventually reach the hump.

The lead was empty of cars, of course, and at the moment there was no activity in the lower yard. Slade paused for a moment to survey his surroundings.

To the left stood a string of cars, perhaps two hundred feet distant. The tracks between the one on which they stood and the lead were unoccupied. Approximately the same condition prevailed to the right. And directly ahead some three score feet a big locomotive stood on the lead purring softly with a full head of steam. The engine crew were not in evidence, doubtless partaking of their lunch at a cook shanty not far off, which was the custom at about this hour.

He was about to continue his trudge up the lead when suddenly, beside the string of cars on his right and a little distance behind, he sensed furtive movement. Another instant and his remarkable eyes made out three barely discernible forms.

Trainmen? No, trainmen wouldn't be lurking in the dark without lanterns. Looked like some gents with notions. Okay, if they were looking for trouble, they'd get it; they'd have to move a mite closer to do any dependable shooting. He loosened the big Colts in their sheaths, cast another look around. And abruptly the situation worsened, decidedly so.

Crouching beside the string of cars on his left were three more vague forms, about the same distance from where he stood as those behind. If the two groups aimed to do a little drygulching, El Halcón was suddenly on a very hot spot. No matter which way he turned, he would be caught in a murderous crossfire, with the odds unpleasantly lopsided. He did some mighty fast thinking.

The locomotive directly ahead? It would provide cover from one group but not from the other, and to even the shelter it promised, it would enable the second group to approach shielded by its bulk; things didn't look at all good.

And then he had an inspiration. He bounded forward and in a trice was beside the steps leading to the engine cab. He whisked up them to the accompaniment of a bellow of guns and a hail of bullets that smacked the tender and the side of the cab. One ripped through his sleeve, just grazing the flesh of his arm. He twirled the sand blowers, slammed the reverse bar down in the corner, released the engine brake and jerked the throttle open, devoutly hoping condensed steam water in the cylinders wouldn't blow a cylinder head.

The stack boomed wetly. The tires ground on the sanded rails, the locomotive lurched forward. More slugs hammered the cab, this time from both sides. Crouching low, Slade peered out the gangway and saw three men running toward the still slowly moving engine, shooting as they came. He whipped out both Colts and squeezed the triggers.

SEVEN

One of the drygulchers rocked back on his heels, reeled sideways and fell to the ground to lie motionless. Before Slade could line sights a second time, the locomotive, picking up speed with every turn of the wheels, had flashed past a string of cars on one of the tracks and hid the target from view. Slade holstered his guns and turned his attention to his iron cayuse that was rocketing down the lead at fifty miles an hour. He thrust his head out the window and gazed ahead.

Lights marking the switches that led from the lead to the car filled tracks were so far all white, meaning the switches were closed. But let one be open and there would be a smashup that would be talked about for some time to come. But he had to distance the three drygulchers on the right before shutting off the steam.

Ahead, at no great distance, showed an ominous red glow. An open switch! Leading to a track almost filled with cars. Slade jammed the throttle shut, applied the brake. The speed lessened, but not enough. He jerked the reverse lever to the rear of the quadrant, hauled the throttle wide open. The bellow of the exhaust joined with the scream of the tortured drive wheels, working in reverse, as they ripped ribbons of steel from the rails.

Peering ahead at that ominous red glow that appeared to be racing toward him, Slade crouched ready to leap from the cab. He heaved a deep breath of relief as, at the very switch points, the locomotive ground to a stop. He closed the throttle, glanced at the water gauge. Plenty of water in the boiler; no danger of an explosion. He dropped from the cab, climbed between two of the cars on the side track, repeated the performance twice more and was out in the open, gazing back up the lead in the hope the drygulchers had followed and would put in an appearance. He wished they would, for now they couldn't surround him and he earnestly desired to even the score for the scare they gave him; riding a runaway locomotive was hard on even El Halcón's nerves.

Far up the lead, lanterns were bobbing about. To Slade's ears came angry shouts. Trainmen were coming to learn what the blankety-blank blue blazes was going on!

The drygulchers did not show, and the lights and the shouts were drawing nearer. With a final glance, Slade hurried from the yard and in another few moments was on a deserted street lined with unlighted warehouses.

After a moment's hesitation, he concluded the Washout would be a good place to hole up for a while, until things had quieted down at the yards. The saloon was some distance away and he didn't think the shooting had been heard there.

Thankful Yates was surprised and pleased at his quick return and at once repaired to the back room for his favorite bottle.

"Thought I'd have one more snort with

you," Slade explained.

They lingered over a drink, until Slade, feeling he had killed enough time, glanced at the clock and said.

"Guess I'd better be heading for the Trail End. Promised the sheriff I'd meet him there for dinner, and if I don't show up soon, he'll be starved and in a bad temper."

When he arrived at the Trail End, Slade was not surprised to find Carter among the absent. He sat down at the table that was always reserved for them and put in his order. Swivel-eye came hurrying to join him.

"Sheriff's over to the railroad yards," he announced.

" 'Pears all hell has busted loose there. Some galoot stole a locomotive and came close to wreckin' it. And they say there's a dead man layin' 'longside the tracks, with a bullet-hole through him. Nobody seems able to figure just what the blazes did happen."

"Chances are the sheriff will find out," El Halcón returned composedly.

"He said to tell you to wait for him here, if you came in," Swivel added, and hustled off to care for his head bartender's demand for stock.

When he arrived, while Slade was eating, the old peace officer wore a strange expres-

64

sion. He sat down and regarded the Ranger in silence for a moment.

"Guess you have something to tell me," he remarked at length. "But first, I've got something to tell *you.*"

"Yes?" Slade prompted.

"Yes. Did you get a good look at that sidewinder you plugged over to the yards?" Carter asked.

"Nope, fortunately I wasn't that close to him and his bunch," Slade returned.

"Well, I did," Carter said. "Who you figure he was?"

Now, Slade had a very good notion as to who he was, but refrained from comment and waited for the sheriff to proceed. Which he did, in the form of a question.

"Remember that hellion who spotted the dead outlaw's carcass in the office this afternoon, said he'd seen him riding with another jigger up to the north of here?"

"I do," Slade admitted.

"Well, that horned toad they found over in the yards is him."

To which information Slade was not at all surprised.

"Why in blazes did he come to the office and do what he did?" wondered Carter.

"Could be several explanations," Slade replied. "Might have been to throw suspicion on Jeff Meader. In which I guess he succeeded, so far as you were concerned. Then again he might have just been keeping tabs on my movements. After what happened, it looks a mite that way. You'll recall I mentioned, while he was there, that I intended to visit the yards later in the evening. Anyhow, there was a very neat trap set for me in the yards. And if that locomotive hadn't been handy, it might well have been successful."

"Tell me about what happened," Carter urged. "Of course, I knew right away that you were mixed up in it somehow."

Slade did so, in detail. The sheriff said a number of things, none of them nice.

"Lucky you know how to handle an engine like you do," he concluded.

"Yes," Slade agreed soberly. "Had a somewhat similar experience once before, down at Sanderson. Used a locomotive in something the same way to prevent a killing and a wreck. Only that time I had a lead switch to the main line set for me and didn't have to worry about slamming into a string of boxcars any minute at fifty miles an hour. Which would probably have served the bunch's purpose as well as a slug between the eyes."

"Oh, sure, only it didn't happen," said the

sheriff. "As usual, some particular devil of your own went along to look after you."

"And as I have said before, he's a nice devil to have along," Slade smiled. The sheriff snorted, then said, "Anyhow, we've started another collection. Six of the hellions done for, which ain't at all bad. A little more and you'll have the whole bunch cleaned up."

"Perhaps, if I cease making blunders like I did today," Slade replied.

"Blunders?"

"Yes. I should have paid more attention to that fellow when he dropped in with his phony yarn, whereas I gave him only cursory thought."

"Well, he fooled me and Grumley, too," the sheriff consoled.

"I'll admit his story had an authentic ring," Slade said. "A very clever bit of work, worthy of our *amigo* Muerto, who is full of surprises."

"Uh-huh, may have been smart, but it didn't work, which is all that really counts," insisted Carter.

"Through no fault of theirs," Slade said. "I just happened to get the breaks."

"I'd say more like you made 'em," the sheriff differed. "Mighty quick thinking on your part."

"You're letting me down easy," Slade laughed. "Well, to paraphrase an old saying, 'Time that grinds the rocks will tell us all!' "

"And I figure you'll give time a hand in the grindin'," the sheriff replied cheerfully. "Well, after I down this surrounding, suppose we amble over to the office and you can have a look at what you bagged."

"A good notion," Slade replied, pushing back his empty plate and rolling a cigarette with the slim fingers of his left hand.

The Trail End was buzzing over the incident in the yards. Wild guesses were tossed back and forth, but nobody appeared able to hit on an explanation.

"Let them guess," Slade said. "And perhaps Muerto is doing a little guessing, too."

"Uh-huh, tryin' to figure how in blazes you caught on like you did," replied Carter. "And now what do you think about Jeff Meader?"

"Would say his position hasn't changed," Slade answered. "Still nothing against him, so far as I can ascertain. And there is a weakness where Meader as a suspect is concerned."

"Yes? What's that?"

"He's too darn obvious and convenient," Slade explained. "So far as we know anything at present, he is a logical suspect. Yes, quite obvious, and I've learned to look with suspicion on the obvious. And if Meader does fade out of the picture, who have we got? Nobody."

"Looks a mite that way," Carter conceded as he shoved back his empty plate. "Well, now for a snort to hold down the surrounding and I'm ready to amble."

A little later they set out for the office, which they reached without incident, to find Deputy Grumley and Tom Balch, his fellow deputy, comfortably ensconced and regarding the blanketed form on the floor complacently.

"Anybody else drop in?" Carter asked.

"Several of the boys from the yards," Grumley replied. "Never saw the horned toad before."

At that moment, a tall, dignified, elderly man entered. It was the General Yardmaster, an old friend of Slade's. He shook hands with the Ranger and twinkled his deep-set eyes.

"Figured you must be in town," he said meaningly. "What do you think of the new Mikado engine we're trying out in the yards?"

"Answers well to the throttle," Slade replied. "Rather heavy for yard work, though, don't you think?"

"Yes, it is," the yardmaster conceded. "We're just trying it out. Will be assigned to a freight run next week. Incidentally, that switch from the lead into a loaded track shouldn't have been left open; somebody's carelessness."

"Glad it wasn't one a little farther up the lead or your wreck crew would be busy about now," Slade said. The yardmaster chuckled.

"Oh, I imagine you would have handled it some way," he said. "Mind telling me just what did happen?"

"Well, seeing as it was in your bailiwick, I guess you have a right to know," Slade answered, and provided details, knowing his hearer was not given to loose talking.

The yardmaster shook his head in mock disapproval. "You're the limit!" he declared. "Just wait till old Jim Dunn hears about this one; he'll blow a gasket."

However, it was doubtful that James G. "Jaggers" Dunn, the famous General Manager of the vast C. & P. Railroad System, would be overly impressed, being accustomed to Slade's escapades, one of which, incidentally, saved the G.M.'s life.

After a little conversation the railroader took his leave. The three law enforcement officers sat sipping coffee and smoking,

70

while on the street outside, Amarillo's roistering night life ebbed and flowed.

Gradually Slade grew restless. Finally he set his empty cup down and stood up.

"I'm going to take another little stroll," he announced. "Think maybe I'll amble down to the Washout. Thankful sometimes gets a rather rough element in his place; might hit on something of interest."

"Mind if I go along?" Carter asked.

"Glad to have you," Slade replied, "to look after me."

"Never mind the sarcasm," the sheriff retorted. "I might come in handy."

"You're right there," Slade agreed soberly, and meant it; the rugged old peace officer was dependable company at all times.

"I remember you used to tease Jerry Norman when you first met her," Carter added. "But she came in mighty handy once."

"You're right there, too," Slade replied. "If she hadn't plugged a drygulcher dead center down in the Canadian Valley, I wouldn't be here talking about it. He had lined sights with me, and my guns were empty. All set to squeeze the trigger, but Jerry's slug got him a split second before his finger tightened."

Jerry Norman was rancher Keith Norman's niece, and half owner of his spread, the biggest and most prosperous in the section. A very presentable young lady, to put it mildly.

"I'll make a point of seeing her in the next few days," Slade said.

"If she's heard you are here, I figure you'll see her even sooner," said Carter. "She'll be heading this way pronto."

"Hope so," Slade said. "I'll be plumb glad to see her."

"She's some gal, all right," the sheriff enthused. "Pretty as a spotted pony, too."

EIGHT

When they reached the Washout and occupied a table, they at once spotted a familiar face. Watson Gaynard, the drilling contractor, was at the far end of the bar talking with Thankful Yates, the owner. They waved a greeting and a few minutes later both crossed to the table and accepted an invitation to take a load off their feet.

"On me this time," said Gaynard. Thankful vetoed the suggestion.

"Nope, on the house," he said. "Hafta keep the sheriff and his deputy oiled or they'll close me up."

"I should anyhow, on general principles,"

replied Carter. "All the time something cuttin' loose in this rumhole. And I might put a charge of tryin' to bribe a law enforcement officer, too."

"Oh, guess a mite of bribin' won't be fatal," Yates said cheerfully as he summoned a waiter.

"Well, Mr. Slade, I at least got the business people to string along with me to the extent of drilling a test well," he said. "I've wired for equipment and an operating crew. Should get started in a few days. I plan to utilize a timber tower rig with a derrick seventy feet high. A boiler furnishes power to the engine. The engine drives a band wheel to which a pitman, or connecting rod, is attached. The pitman works a walking beam supported by a Samson post, a post of great strength. To the other end of the walking beam the string of drilling tools is attached. The cable which holds the tools is wound around a bull wheel at the base of the derrick and passes over a crown pulley at the top. As the walking beam jigs up and down, the bit at the end of the string of tools rises and falls, boring into the earth.

"I know this sounds technical," he concluded apologetically, "but the operation is really quite simple, as you will agree when you see it."

"Sounds very interesting," Slade said, vaguely. "Have you decided where you will drill your well?"

"Yes, I have," Gaynard replied. "A little to the southwest of Amarillo Lake."

Slade's eyes narrowed the merest trifle, but he did not comment.

A few moments later, Gaynard pushed aside his empty glass and stood up.

"Have to be going," he said. "A busy day tomorrow. Thanks for the drink, Yates." With a nod and a smile he walked out.

"A nice feller," said Thankful. " 'Pears to know his business, too."

"Yes, it appears that way," Slade agreed.

"Think he'll get water?" the sheriff asked.

"Yes, he'll get water, all right," Slade replied. Something in the tone of his voice caused Carter to shoot him a glance. But El Halcón did not comment further.

"Sounded mighty complicated, the way he explained it," Yates remarked.

"Yes, the way he explained it," Slade agreed. "Really, however, the operation is quite simple. The weight bit rises and falls as the rope to which it is suspended unwinds from the drum, boring into the earth by its steady impact, much like driving a stake into the ground. The walking beam is the same as a teeter-totter, or see-saw, kids play with, one end rising, the other falling, the process repeated over and over. That's really all there is to it."

"The way you explain it, anybody can understand it," chuckled Yates. He glanced around the room.

"Sorta slow tonight, but to be expected, with payday for the spreads and the railroads only a coupla days off. Things will pick up then, and I ain't joking."

The sheriff downed a final snort, also glanced around, and at the clock.

"Suppose we call it a night, Walt," he suggested.

"A notion," Slade agreed. "Has been a busy day."

The following morning, Slade took another walk, to the edge of Amarillo Lake. For some time he stood gazing across it, noting that there was a slight but steady swirl on its placid surface, near the center, and turned his attention to the creek which emptied into it, the concentration furrow deep between his black brows. A sure sign El Halcón was doing some hard thinking. Finally, with a shrug of his broad shoulders, he made his way to the sheriff's office, where Doc Beard planned to hold an inquest on the body of the mysteriously slain dryglucher.

The only witnesses called were railroaders who discovered the body, and they had nothing to add to what was already known, that the gentleman in question was thoroughly dead, with, the jury intimated, nothing lost to the community, judging from the looks of him.

"Anyhow, a nice fat passel of *dinero* in his pockets," the sheriff remarked cheerfully. "More than the hellion ever earned swinging a loop. Cowhand, all right, wouldn't you say, Walt?"

"Marks of rope and branding iron on his hands, none recent, tend to indicate he once was," El Halcón replied. "Guess he turned to other pursuits, quite a while back."

"And guess his other *pursuits* took a turn for the worse," was the sheriff's comment. With which nobody disagreed.

"And now what's in order?" Carter asked.

"It's not late, and I think I'll ride over and visit old Estaban who lives in the Valley down this way," Slade replied. "He has influence in the Valley and there isn't much going on he doesn't know about. And after I leave him, I may ride on to Keith Norman's place."

"Then I won't see you till tomorrow or tomorrow night, yes?"

"Guess so," Slade agreed. "I'll be back not later than tomorrow night. I want to be here for the payday bust. Something of interest may happen then."

"Will sure be unusual if something doesn't," the sheriff grunted disgustedly. "Never knew it to fail. Okay, be seeing you when I do."

Cinching up, Slade rode north through a beautiful early autumn day. Shadow, glad of a chance to stretch his legs, stepped out briskly, the miles flowing back under his speeding irons.

Continually, Slade swept the prairie with his gaze. Almost always it lay lonely and devoid of life save for occasional clumps of grazing cows, and birds flitting about. A couple of times he saw, in the distance, cowhands checking cattle, for the beef roundup was drawing near. He did not approach them but rode steadily.

As he approached the Valley, the sun lay low over the lonely rangeland and glittered on the fringe of growth that clothed the Valley lip, turning withered leaves into flakes of dead gold, the brighter for the shadowy depths of chaparral behind them.

As he looked upon the autumnal scene and marveled at its beauty, the thought came to Slade that decay can be as fair as growth, and death as life, to the seeing eye. He rode on, his spirit uplifted.

Without difficulty, on sure-footed Shadow, he negotiated the descent to the Valley floor. The sun had set and the lovely blue dusk was sifting into the great depression like impalpable dust. He turned west and after covering a couple of miles he rounded a bend and before him lay a clearing in which stood a tight and well cared for adobe cabin surrounded by a flourishing garden patch. Nearby grazed a respectable number of sheep and goats. Smoke rose from the mud and stick chimney and through the open door, mingling with the tang of burning wood, came a most delectable odor, more fragrant to the olfactory nerves of a hungry man than all the spices of Arabia, the smell of cooking meat and boiling coffee.

As Slade rode up to the cabin, a sprightly old Mexican with snow-white hair and a wrinkled face appeared in the doorway. He peered with bright black eyes, gave a glad cry and came running to grasp the hand Slade held down to him.

"*Capitán!* Again you return to Estaban!" he chattered joyfully. "Ha! And the beautiful *caballo,* too!" With a pat for Shadow's glossy neck. "Dismount, *Capitán,* dismount! To the stable he goes, to company keep with my mule, Carmencita, and with oats be stuffed to the bursting. Then for us a feast fit to the occasion."

Shadow was domiciled beside the pensive-looking Carmencita, all his wants cared for. Then Estaban led the way to the cabin, chattering volubly in his Mission-taught English, with an occasional Spanish word thrown in.

"You I have expected, *Capitán,*" he said as he poured Slade a cup of steaming coffee. "Up and down the Valley the word has gone that El Halcón is here, and that El Halcón says that Muerto, formerly a name of dread is but a ruthless *bandido* as vulnerable to a well placed bullet as any other *ladrone.* The people believe, and no longer fear Muerto as an evil spirit risen from the dead. They watch and they wait, and it will be an evil day indeed for Muerto do they the chance get to, as *Capitán* would say, line sights with him."

"And that helps a lot," Slade said. "And I've a notion you had considerable of a hand in spreading the word."

Estaban's oblique reply admitted as much, "It is the honor great to be of service to El Halcón." Humming gaily, he got busy at the stove.

When the meal was ready, it proved to be

all Estaban claimed it would be, and Slade did it full justice.

"Yes, dispelling the illusion that Muerto is something more than human is a big help," he said as he rolled a cigarette. "But don't discount him. He's a shrewd, resourceful and merciless devil, and not given to making many slips."

"The slip he will make, the one too many," Estaban declared confidently. "Into a grave he will slip, nor will he come out again. Not until the last trumpet sounds and he will stand naked and alone before the Last Judgment."

"Here's hoping you're right," Slade smiled.

"I am right," Estaban replied. "*Capitán* never fails." Slade changed the subject.

"Have cows passed across the Valley of late, do you know?" he asked. Estaban shook his head.

"Here none pass," he said. "But to the west of Tascosa, many have entered the Valley from the north to — vanish."

"You mean they continue west by way of the Valley? Not many herders over there, I know, but it looks like they would have been observed."

"The herders say they do not follow the Valley, but disappear once they enter it.

80

With them those who drove them. It has strengthened the Muerto myth. The herders say that no man of honest flesh and blood could vanish that way, with him all that accompany him, even beasts."

Slade was not impressed by the loco yarn. The great Valley had its secrets, geological and otherwise. Doubtless there was a hidden and little-known way up the south cliffs to the west, and then a straight shoot to the New Mexico hills and the buyers. A herd could make it in a single night of fast driving.

For some time, Slade sat smoking and thinking, while Estaban watched him in silence. He considered what he had learned to be of value. Might well provide opportunity to set a trap for the wideloopers. That is, if he could discover the route by which they left the Valley

Estaban poured more coffee and produced a husk *cigarillo* which he lighted. He blew out smoke and broke the silence, "*Capitán* plans?"

"Yes, I do," Slade admitted. "The prevalent belief among the ranchers is that the stolen cattle reached the New Mexico line by way of the Valley. They patrol the land over there and have set traps, so far without intercepting the rustlers. The answers being that the cows do not reach the Line by way of the Valley."

"So it would seem," Estaban conceded.

A period of silence followed, which finally Slade broke.

"Estaban," he said, "I'm going to play a hunch."

"And *Capitán's* hunches are straight ones," interpolated the Mexican.

"Anyhow, I'm going to play it," El Halcón continued. "Tomorrow is payday for the spreads. Tonight most of the patrols will be called in and things will be lax. Which might possibly provide the wideloopers with the opportunity to run off a few head of stock. So I'll give my horse another hour to rest and digest his oats, then I'm riding west."

"It will be dangerous, *Capitán,* with the odds against you," Estaban protested.

"I'll risk it," Slade replied. "I don't intend to get mixed up in a ruckus if I can help it. What I hope to do is find out how the cows leave the Valley. Then there's a chance to set a real trap for the galoots."

"That is so," Estaban admitted, "*Vaya usted con Dios* — go you with God."

The hour passed. Slade got the rig on Shadow, who appeared to be in fine fettle, and headed up the Valley. He detoured the

82

Quijano cabin, a few miles farther on; somebody there might have a loose trigger finger. Moreover, he did not wish to have his ride interrupted. Regaining the trail, he continued at a brisk pace.

The night was clear, the stars burning brightly. The Valley was deathly still, with no sign of life. Without incident he passed several small plazas where sheep grazed, the cabins dark. Bypassing Tascosa, he rode on for another ten miles then, at a point known to him, he ascended to the prairie.

Now the hills of New Mexico were in view, with the Tucumcari Mountains, that looked like the breasts of a sleeping woman, looming far to the west, the pitiless Tucumcari Desert lying between the mountains and north Texas.

In a convenient thicket not far from the Valley lip, he holed up, loosening the cinches and flipping out the bit for Shadow's comfort, made himself as comfortable as conditions would permit, and settled down to rest. And meanwhile the hunch was growing stronger by the minute.

The hours dragged on. The great clock in the sky wheeled westward. And Slade grew heartily weary of the interminable wait, and began to wonder were he following a cold trail.

And then his patience was at long last rewarded. Faint and thin with distance sounded the querulous plaint of a tired and disgusted steer.

Slade stiffened to attention. Quickly he tightened the cinches, flipped the bit back into place, and stood gazing northward whence the sound came. Yes, his hunch was a straight one. A herd was being shoved to the Valley.

Mounting Shadow, he eased him to the edge of the thicket, making sure his guns were smooth in their sheaths.

Louder and louder grew the sound of the approaching cows. A few more moments and his keen eyes made out the moving shadow that was the herd, which he quickly estimated to number around fifty head. He fingered the butt of his rifle uncertainly. With the long-range Winchester and his speedy horse, he might be able to so harass the wideloopers that they would abandon the cattle before reaching the safety of the descent.

That would save the herd, but would defeat his main objective, which was to ascertain how the critters were shoved out of the Valley without being detected. He arrived at a decision.

The stolen beefs very likely belonged to

John Fletcher or Keith Norman, either of which could absorb the loss. He figured the end he hoped for would justify the means. Relaxing, he waited.

On came the cows. A little later they were streaming past Slade's thicket, half a dozen riders shoving them along. Slade wished the light were better so he could distinguish faces, which at that distance were but whitish blurs.

Straight for the descent by which he had reached the prairie the herd was pushed, to vanish from sight amid the growth, the riders following.

Slade waited until he was sure both beefs and riders had reached the Valley floor. Then he sent Shadow forward. He desired to keep distance between him and the quarry. Odds of six to one were a bit lopsided, did a corpse and cartridge session ensue.

His keen ears told him exactly which direction the herd was taking, south by a little west. Soon he figured they must be nearing the south wall, the Valley being somewhat narrow here. He quickened Shadow's pace a little.

Abruptly the sounds became stationary. El Halcón curbed his mount a bit and rode alert and watchful. Now he could dimly make out the towering cliffs of the Valley wall.

The racket kicked up by the cows again developed movement. But the sound dimmed quickly. A few more moments and it faded to silence.

"Now what in blazes?" wondered the mystified Ranger. The only answer appeared to be that the weary cows were climbing the steep ascent from the Valley and were saving their breath for the trudge. Which seemed highly unusual, to put it mildly.

His curiosity at a white heat, Slade recklessly speeded up, his gaze sweeping the cliff face, back and forth. He could not make out the least sign of a way up the sheer wall, the base of which was heavily grown with tall and thick chaparral.

Within half a dozen yards of the rock wall, he drew rein in a last protecting straggle of brush. There was not a cow in sight. Nor a sign of the six wideloopers. The Valley lay as silent and deserted as at Creation's dawn.

Leaving the brush, he rode back and forth along the rock wall, studying it with a carping eye, and discovering nothing. The cliffs were sheer, unbroken, even overhanging at places. If there was a way up them, ocular demonstration failed to ascertain it.

"Blast it, Shadow, it almost makes one

inclined to agree with the herders that there is something supernatural about that devil's antics," he complained. "Well, he sure put one over on us. No sense in trying to learn how tonight. Daylight may be another story."

Thoroughly disgusted with the results, or lack of results, of his pilgrimage, he headed back down the Valley.

The sun was well up when Slade reached Estaban's cabin. The old Mexican took one look at him and said, "*Capitán,* your eyes are heavy, your face weary. To bed with you, in the little room where you slept before. Of the *caballo* I care."

Too tired to argue, Slade stretched out on the comfortable bunk and was almost immediately sound asleep.

It was close to noon when he awoke. Estaban had his breakfast ready for him. For his host's benefit, he recounted his misadventures of the night before.

"And you have no idea as to how the *ganado* left the Valley?" Estaban asked.

"I have a vague theory," Slade replied. "Hope to put it to the test before long. Right now I'm heading for Amarillo. *Gracias* for everything. You are a real *amigo.*"

"I am honored," Estaban answered, reverently bowing his white head.

Watchful and alert, Slade left the Valley. Upon reaching the crest, he searched the prairie in all directions with his eyes. Satisfied with what he didn't see, he reached the trail and rode south at a fast pace.

When he reached Amarillo, the payday celebration was in full swing. Lines of cow ponies stood at the racks, their riders crowding the saloons, restaurants and shops, and more hands were riding in by the minute. All day the railroaders had been filing past the paycar window and were doing their best to make the bust a success, with evidence they wouldn't fail in their endeavor. Music and a babble of talk blasted over the swinging doors. The sidewalks were crowded with an already boisterous throng.

After caring for his horse, Slade made his way to the sheriff's office. He had barely entered the door when he was seized from behind, his arms pinned to his sides.

NINE

Sheriff Carter, composedly occupying his chair, made no move to assist him.

In fact, Slade didn't try very hard to free himself from the slender encircling arms. He merely twisted around enough to gaze down into an elfinly beautiful little heart-shaped face with great dark eyes and red, red lips.

"You imp!" he said. "Up to your old tricks, eh?" Her arms were burst asunder, hands cupped her tiny waist and she was tossed into the air.

Miss Jerry Norman shrieked as her curly dark head almost touched the ceiling and her skirt whisked up knee-high and more.

But he deftly caught her before her feet struck the floor, and held her close.

"I wanted to surprise you," she breathlessly panted. "Might have known you'd do something outlandish to even up. I figured I'd collect a broken neck at least. You scared me out of my p-poise!"

The sheriff shook with laughter.

"I told you you'd be sorry if you hid behind the door," he reminded her.

He and Jerry listened with avid interest to Slade's account of the vanished cattle. Carter muttered under his mustache. Jerry sighed and shook her curly head.

"I wouldn't be surprised if they were some of our stock," she said. "But thank goodness you didn't charge all six of those killers, trying to get them back."

"Figures it would not be the wisest course to follow, and besides I felt learning how they were gotten out of the Valley was more important."

"And you've no notion how they did it?" Carter asked.

Slade's reply was much the same as his answer to Estaban's similar question, "I have a theory, that's all."

The sheriff looked receptive, but El Halcón did not choose to elaborate at the moment.

The door opened and old Keith Norman, Jerry's uncle, stalked in to shake hands warmly with Slade.

"So the tyke found you, eh?" he chuckled. "When we rode in, Brian told us you were out gallivantin' somewhere but that he expected you back before dark. Mighty glad you made it. What's new?"

Slade repeated the story of the night's incidents. Norman nodded his grizzled head sagely.

"You'll find out how they do it, no doubt as to that," he said. "Just a matter of time."

"I'm hungry," Jerry announced.

"When ever wasn't you?" her uncle retorted. "Keep on at the rate you're going and you'll end up so fat you'll waddle like a duck, eh, Walt?"

"I would say she has a long ways to go," Slade smiled, with an appreciative glance at Jerry's proportions, which he considered well nigh perfect. She wasn't very big, but what there was of her certainly left nothing to be desired.

"Feeling a mite lank myself," said the sheriff. "Suppose we amble over to the Trail End and tie onto a surrounding."

When they reached the Trail End, they found it crowded to bursting at the seams, but Swivel-eye had a table reserved for them. He waved a greeting and hurried to the kitchen to notify the cook.

"This is wonderful," enthused Jerry as they sat down. "I love paydays; they're always so exciting."

"Too darned exciting at times," grumbled the sheriff taking a hearty sip of the snort the waiter placed before him.

But there was a gleam in his frosty eyes that caused Slade to smile. Brian Carter was sorta old, but he still enjoyed a mite of excitement.

"Later I want you to take me to that nice place, the Washout, Walt," said Jerry. "Uncle Keith never will."

"That rumhole!" snorted Norman. "The bunch in there is enough to give a person the creeps. Hardly a one of 'em good for anything but to stretch rope."

"I think they're nice," differed Jerry. "And Mr. Yates is wonderful."

"Oh, he ain't so bad," Norman admitted. "Keeps pretty good order, too, considerin' what he has to deal with. Well, here comes our surrounding. About time, I feel the need of it."

The dinner proved to be excellent, and after they had finished eating, even Jerry admitted she wasn't hungry any more.

"And I'm going to be really reckless and top it off with a glass of wine," she announced.

"Which inspires me to the extent of a snort," said the sheriff. Old Keith applauded the notion and went along with it. Slade settled for a final cup of coffee and a cigarette.

Norman moved to the bar to talk with some people he knew. Young Joyce Echols, one of the XT hands, asked Jerry to dance. Slade and Carter were left to their smokes and a little serious conversation.

"And you really figure you can hit on how those hellions run the cows outa the Valley?" Carter asked.

"Yes, I think I can," Slade replied. "If it's what I think it is, I'll have to give somebody credit for exceeding shrewness and a surprising knowledge of a certain sort. Wait till I try it out and I'll tell you all about it. And if things work as I hope they will, we'll have a good chance to give the devils a wallop they'll remember for some time. With a little luck we may knock off the head of the bunch."

"Speaking of the head of the bunch, if the devils have got a way out of the Valley nobody knows about, it sorta eliminates Jeff Meader, meaning that the cows ain't run across his Triangle M spread, doesn't it?" asked the sheriff.

"Not necessarily," Slade answered. "It is still possible that stock could be run across his land during the night, with the wide-loopers knowing of a spot where they can be holed up in the daytime and when darkness falls, shoved across to the hills. Would be a long drive over a bad terrain, but it could be done by men who are capable, know their business, and are familiar with topographical peculiarities of the section. So Meader mustn't be altogether ruled out at present. It would be a hazardous drive, but I repeat, it could be done."

"But I got a feeling you don't believe it is done," the sheriff remarked shrewdly. Slade smiled, and did not further commit himself.

Carter glanced around the roaring room, growled and shook his head.

"A wild one tonight, for fair," he said. "The sorta night anything can happen. If some hellishness don't cut loose 'fore it's over, I miss my guess."

Studying the hilarious crowd that was growing more boisterous by the minute, El Halcón was inclined to agree. Without doubt, other places were also going strong, and not all were as orderly as the Trail End usually was with a little mild persuading on the part of Swivel-eye and his gentle floor men who were adept in the wielding of sawed-off baseball bats they kept tucked under their belts. He wondered how the Washout was making out. Thankful Yates was also good at persuading belligerent gentlemen to curb their warlike tendencies, but he did get a rougher crowd than did the Trail End.

Well, he'd very likely find out, for Jerry was set on visiting the lakefront place and he considered it easier to accede to her wishes than argue with her.

"Look!" the sheriff suddenly exclaimed. "Here comes Jeff Meader, and he's got three of his young hellions with him. Ornery-looking coots, don't you think?"

Slade smiled, and did not commit himself. In fact, the Triangle M rannies appeared to him to be average young cowhands of their type, ready for a fight, a frolic, or a footrace, or anything that promised entertainment or excitement. Probably with little real harm in them, but easily led by a more dominant personality, perhaps along a trail that would not be of their own choosing.

That the rugged Jeff Meader was such a personality Slade was willing to concede. However, that did not necessarily mean he went in for off-color practices, or would condone such in his employees. Everything considered, Meader was something of an enigma, and as such, of interest to El Halcón.

Meader and his men nudged their way to the bar, where they stood drinking and talking. Slade studied the rancher's face, and arrived at certain conclusions which he did not vocalize.

Another familiar face appeared at the door. It was Watson Gaynard, the drilling promoter. He glanced around, waved to Slade and the sheriff and managed a place at the bar.

"Clothes are dusty, looks like he's been doing some riding," Carter remarked.

"Yes, he does," Slade agreed thoughtfully, eyeing Gaynard's dusty coat.

Gaynard didn't stay long. He had a couple of drinks, waved again, and departed. Slade's eyes, still thoughtful, followed his progress to the swinging doors.

"Wonder if he's looking for still another spot to sink a well?" said Carter.

"It is possible," Slade replied.

Jerry came bounding over from the dance floor, her cheeks rosy, her eyes sparkling.

"I want another sip of wine and then I want to go to the Washout," she announced.

"Mind if I go along?" asked Carter. "Keith and those old fossils he's gabbin' with will be at it all night."

"Be glad to have you, Uncle Brian," Jerry instantly answered. "Maybe you can keep Walt out of trouble."

"More likely he'll leave me to take care of you and go gallivantin' off looking for some," predicted the sheriff. "Down your snort and we'll get goin'."

Jerry did so and they set out, worming their way through the hilarious throng that packed the board sidewalks and spilled out onto the street, regardless of the cowhands racing their horses along it. However, they managed to reach the lakefront in one piece.

The Trail End had been wild, but tame compared to the Washout, where everybody appeared to be yelling at once and with but one object in mind, to get drunk as quickly and thoroughly as possible.

So far, however, all was gaiety and good humor.

"But just wait," growled Carter. "Just wait till the red-eye begins to really get in its licks. There'll be a full-fledged riot here before the night is over, or I miss my guess."

Thankful Yates hurried to join them, grinning broadly and voicing a hearty welcome.

"Figured you'd show up and saved a table for you," he said, "the one Mr. Slade likes." He led the way to it, beckoning a waiter.

A table, incidentally, from which El Halcón had a view of the door and the windows, and most of the room as reflected in the back bar mirror.

"Now this is something like," said Jerry. "The Trail End is quite stodgy by comparison."

"And a darn sight safer," grumbled the sheriff. "Fill 'em up, I feel the need of a flock of snorts, after a look at this rumhole."

"I'll risk one more small glass of wine," Jerry said. Slade again settled for coffee and studied the occupants of the room. Mostly a regulation payday crowd, although there were a few individuals he was not too sure about, was his conclusion.

After she had finished her wine, Jerry jumped to her feet.

"Come on, Walt, and dance with me," she said.

"Dance, on that floor!" Slade protested.

"There isn't room to more than shuffle."

"Which just means you hold your partner closer," Jerry giggled. "Come on!"

Walt Slade liked to dance, and he could dance. So could Jerry Norman. Gradually the other couples edged away from them to watch their performance, and when they left the floor there was a round of applause, in which Thankful Yates joined heartily.

"I'd sure like to hire you both to put one on every night," he said. "Would keep the place packed."

"And just wait until I persuade him to sing," said Jerry.

"That's right," agreed Thankful, "the sing-ingest man in the whole Southwest.

"And with the fastest gunhand," he added as an afterthought.

Carter gave vent to a disgusted snort. "Was bad enough already, now it's worse," he growled. "Here comes Meader and his galoots."

The Triangle M owner found a place at the bar. His rannies drifted to the dance floor, where they quickly acquired partners. Meader stood sipping his drink, and gazed into the back bar mirror. Slade was pretty sure that once or twice his glance glinted toward the table he and his companions oc-cupied.

Meanwhile, Slade was growing restless. Kale Fenton, another of the XT punchers who, with a couple of others, had followed them to the Washout, asked Jerry to dance. She complied. Slade stood up.

"I hanker to have a look outside," he told Carter. "You stay here and keep an eye on Jerry, please. I'll be back shortly."

"Okay," replied the sheriff. "Watch your step." Slade moved toward the door. At that moment, Meader shoved his empty glass aside, glanced at the clock and walked out. Slade was but a few steps behind him.

TEN

Outside, a gun cracked, followed by a cry of pain. Slade whipped a Colt from its sheath and bounded through the swinging doors to see Jeff Meader, blood streaming down his face, fighting furiously with three men. He saw the gleam of a raised knife and lashed out with the Colt. The heavy barrel crunched on a wrist. The knife fell to the ground. Its owner howled with pain.

Another underhand slashing blow laid a second man's cheek open to the bone, slamming him against the building wall. He recovered and all three took to their heels down the street.

Slade lined sights, but held his fire. He didn't know what it was all about and anyhow the situation appeared to be under control. Besides, there were people on the street, in line. He turned to Meader who was leaning against the wall, gasping and swabbing at the blood that flowed from a cut in his forehead just in front of the temple.

"You all right?" Slade asked.

"Just nicked," the rancher panted. "Sorta knocked me silly for a minute."

"Inside, and we'll take care of it," Slade told him as Sheriff Carter came bursting through the door, gun in hand, after him Jerry Norman, also with a gun in her hand.

"To the back room, Brian," Slade said.

The sheriff whirled and began shouldering his way through the crowd that was pressing toward the door. He was quickly reinforced by the three XT hands and Meader's punchers, who had come rushing forward. Jerry followed close behind Slade, who supported Meader, the gun in her hand swinging back and forth, waist high, and causing a scattering on the part of those who noticed the hammer was at full cock.

Thankful Yates, whose composure it seemed nothing could shake, flung open the door to the back room.

"Got everything you'll need, Mr. Slade, always have 'em, as you know," he said cheerfully, drawing ointment and bandage rolls from a drawer. "Here's a chair, Mr. Meader. Squat."

Confident the wound was of little consequence, Slade quickly had it padded and bandaged, the flow of blood curbed. He cleaned the rancher's face with a damp towel Thankful procured, rolled and lighted a cigarette and handed it to him.

"That should hold you until the doctor has a look," he said. "And now, Mr. Meader, suppose you tell us what it was all about."

"I'll be hanged if I know," Meader replied, dragging hard on the cigarette. "I stepped out the door and a hellion shoved a gun right in my face and fired pointblank. I ducked in time and knocked the gun out of his hand before he could shoot a second time. Then the three of them were all over me. I guess you saved me from getting a knife slit in my hide," he added with a grateful glance at Slade.

"Possibly," the Ranger admitted. "Did you know those fellows?"

"Never saw them before in my life," Meader declared. "And I can't imagine who would want to murder me. I've had a few ruckuses with fellers, but none of them the sort who would do a thing like that."

"This section is full of sidewinders that would shoot a man just for the fun of it," growled the sheriff.

"Can he have a drink, Mr. Slade?" Thankful asked, appearing with a full glass in his hand.

"As many as he wishes," Slade replied. Meader gave him another grateful look, and emptied the glass.

"Well, looks like everything is under control," Slade said. "Let's go, Jerry."

"And Jerry, where the blazes did you get that gun, and what did you do with it?" Carter asked.

"Never you mind," Miss Norman retorted. "I can get it again if I need it."

"Hmmm!" said the sheriff. "Guess it's lucky you're wearing a long dress tonight."

Jerry wrinkled her pert nose at him and refused to rise to the bait.

"Just a minute, Mr. Slade," Meader requested as he stood up, his punchers clustering watchfully around him.

"I'd — I'd like to shake hands with you," he added diffidently.

"A pleasure," Slade replied. Their hands met in a hearty grip.

Making their way through the buzzing,

questioning crowd, they finally reached their table.

"If he was telling the truth about never seeing those horned toads before, what in blazes *was* it all about?" Carter wondered.

"I can't say for sure, of course," Slade answered thoughtfully, "but I've a feeling it could very well have been a case of mistaken identity."

"Meaning?"

"Meaning that Meader is very nearly my height, and plenty broad. And in a dim light, one big man looks much the same as another."

"You mean it was you they were after?" asked the startled sheriff.

"So I assume," Slade said. "Doubtless they were waiting and watching outside the door, saw me stand up and start for the door and got all set for business. But Meader was a couple of steps ahead of me and they went for him."

Jerry shuddered. Carter muttered things under his mustache.

"Well," he said aloud, "those three sidewinders may not know it, but they were plumb lucky. If they'd tried to jump you that way, right now we'd have three carcasses to deal with."

Slade laughed, and didn't argue the point.

"So we still don't know exactly where Meader stands," the sheriff observed.

"About the size of it," Slade conceded, "although he does appear to be gradually fading out of the picture. Of one thing I am convinced, he has nothing to do with running cows across the Valley and out of the Valley by a hidden route. Which tends to discount him as being Muerto; he just doesn't fill the bill."

"One thing is sure for certain, though. He has a quick mind and a fast hand, which enabled him to instantly size up the situation, duck out of line in the split second before the drygulcher squeezed trigger, and slap the gun out of his hand before he could fire a second time. An able man and, I would say, adept at anything to which he may turn."

"Blast it!" the sheriff grumbled querulously, "first you just about put the hellion in the clear, then you come up with something that sets a feller wondering again.

"Oh, I suppose sooner or later you'll drop a loop on somebody nobody else has given a thought to; won't be the first time."

Slade smiled, and asked Jerry if she would have more wine.

For a while the abortive attempt on Jeff Meader's life was the chief topic of conversation, but not for too long, there being other things to occupy the celebrants' minds. Such as drinks, cards, and dancefloor girls. Soon the Washout was back to its normal state of payday heck raising.

Carter's two deputies dropped in with no serious incidents to report, so far. A few mild ruckuses, but nothing to get excited about. They accepted a drink and ambled out for a look at the lakefront places.

"Wouldn't be surprised if the larrupin' you gave those two devils sorta cooled down the bunch for tonight," the sheriff observed to Slade.

"Here's hoping," the Ranger replied. "I feel I can do with a little peace and quiet for a change."

"And right now we're going to have some real music for a change," said Jerry.

She jumped to her feet, trotted through the crowd to where Yates stood and engaged him in conversation.

Thankful smiled and nodded and spoke to the orchestra leader, who grinned and bobbed delightedly and waved a guitar over his head.

"Guess you know what that means," Carter chuckled.

"Reckon I do," Slade replied resignedly. He moved to the little raised platform that accommodated the musicans, voiced a Spanish greeting that caused their smiles to broaden, and accepted the guitar.

"Silence!" bellowed Thankful. "Silence, please!"

All faces turned to the platform. Those who knew what to expect nudged others to keep quiet.

Booming chords from the guitar, a soft prelude, and El Halcón threw back his black head and sang.

And as his great golden bass-baritone rolled in thunder through the room, sank to a whisper of exquisite melody, soared and pealed again, his audience stood entranced.

Songs these rugged men understood and loved. Songs of the hills and the valleys, of the rivers and the plains, of the glowing campfire and the sleeping herd. And ever the lonely horseman riding the lonely trail that wound over the rim of the world.

Simple songs, but fraught with a grand simplicity that quickened the mind of the dullest and freed imagination to climb the stairway of the heavens and juggle with the stars!

After each number a storm of applause, and shouts for another.

In conclusion, a smile for the dance-floor girls, a wistful love song of haunting beauty that brought filmy hankerchiefs into play.

A ripple of melody from the guitar, born of the crisp power of a master's touch, and he returned the instrument to its owner, bowed acknowledgment to the continued applause and sauntered back to his table, where Jerry Norman sat with tears gemming her dark lashes.

"Wonderful!" she murmured. "Wonderful, as always, and always the outward trail!"

"But he'll come riding back," predicted the old sheriff. "Can't stay away."

"Yes," replied Jerry, "but the days of waiting are lonely."

"A glass of wine will help," chuckled Carter as he beckoned a waiter.

"And now," Jerry suggested, after she finished her wine, "don't you think we'd better return to the Trail End for a while? Poor Mr. Sanders will think we've deserted him. And it is getting late."

"A good idea," Slade agreed. Carter seconded the motion.

They stood up and waved good night to Thankful. Jeff Meader hurried from the bar to join them.

"Just want to thank you again, Mr. Slade, for everything, including your marvelous singing," he said. "If I could sing like that, I wouldn't care a haycock to be President."

"I'm glad it pleased you," Slade replied. "How does your head feel?"

"Fine, thanks to you," Meader answered. "Doesn't hurt a bit."

"Drop in and see Doc Beard tomorrow," Slade advised.

"Okay," Meader agreed, "but I've a notion you are as good at patchin' up folks as Doc himself."

"Doc has said as much," the sheriff put in.

"I don't doubt it," said Meader.

"Just the same, drop in and see him," Slade repeated. "It isn't wise to take chances with a head wound. And anyhow he'll want to change the pad and bandage. Good night."

As they jostled their way through the crowd on the street, the sheriff remarked, "Well, if that jigger isn't all right, he's sure one good actor." Slade nodded agreement.

Slade was watchful as they walked, although he didn't really expect any more trouble. But as he told Meader apropos of his head, best not to take chances. Not with a hellion like Muerto, who was as tenacious of purpose as he was resourceful.

However, they reached the Trail End without incident, to find it had quieted down somewhat for tired nature was taking toll, and there was work to do tomorrow.

"Don't see Uncle Keith?" Jerry remarked, glancing around. "I imagine he headed for bed long ago; he was up at daybreak."

Which Swivel-eye confirmed when he joined them for a moment, a little later.

"And, Walt, I think we'd better call it a night," Jerry said.

"Registered at the same hotel?" the sheriff asked innocently.

Jerry made a face at him.

Eleven

Old Keith and his niece rode to their spread early the following afternoon.

"But we'll be back in a few days," Jerry told Slade. "And perhaps you'll be able to make it to the casa soon."

"I expect to," the Ranger replied.

"And now what's the line-up?" Carter asked as they sat in the office sipping coffee and smoking.

"I think late tonight I'll ride to the Valley," Slade replied. "I'll hole up for a few hours under a bush. I wish to look things over by daylight."

"Figure you'll be all right?" Carter asked, a worried wrinkle between his brows.

"No reason why I shouldn't be," Slade

said. "I aim to slip out of town after dark, and nobody can follow me across the prairie without me spotting them."

"Okay," said the sheriff, "but watch your step. It's safe to say you are a long ways from being popular with certain gents about now, including one with a busted wrist and another one with a busted face."

"Doesn't matter, just so I'm not unpopular with the right sort of folks," Slade replied cheerfully.

Slade and the sheriff enjoyed a leisurely late dinner at the Trail End. For a time they sat and talked. Then Slade repaired to his hotel room. Without lighting the lamp, he drew a chair to the window and for an hour smoked and gazed at the star glow. Finally he slipped quietly from the hotel, cinched up and rode north out of town.

"Well, feller, here goes for a try at learning something," he told Shadow. "Sort of playing a hunch, as it were, but not altogether. For after thinking things over, I've a very good notion as to what we are going to find. So june along, horse, we've got things to do."

Shadow, who didn't like being cooped up, snorted agreement and forged ahead at a fast pace.

For some time, Slade scanned the back

110

trail. The sky was brilliant with stars and objects were visible for quite some distance. However, there were no objects to be seen on the treeless plain, not even to the eyes of El Halcón. So he faced to the front and headed for the Canadian Valley.

He did not linger in the great depression, once he reached it, but rode straight across and ascended the north wall to the rangeland and continued west, not drawing rein until he reached the point a few hours before daybreak where the widelooped cows had been run into the Valley, to vanish.

Again he descended to the Valley floor, located a little cleared space near the river bank where grass grew, and which was surrounded by chaparral. He stripped off the rig so Shadow could graze in comfort, rolled up in his blanket with his saddle for a pillow and was quickly asleep.

The carolling of birds in the thickets awakened him before daybreak. He had stowed some staple provisions in his saddle pouches. So he kindled a tiny fire of dry wood, confident the trickle of smoke would not be noticeable in the gray light. He procured water from the nearby river and set about preparing breakfast. Soon coffee was bubbling in a little flat bucket, bacon and eggs sizzling in a small skillet. Which with a hunch of bread took care of all the needs of the inner man. Shadow made out with a helping of oats from one of the pouches to hold down the foundation of grass he had already laid.

After cleaning and stowing the utensils, Slade rolled a cigarette, stretched out on his blanket and enjoyed a leisurely smoke to the tunes of the little feathered songsters who were flitting about in search of their own breakfast.

He was in no hurry and it was well past daybreak when he cinched up, forded the river and with unerring instinct followed the course taken by the vanishing wide-looped cows a few nights before.

He rode slowly but steadily, and after a while the beetling cliffs of the south wall came into view. For some moments he scanned them with interest, and when the trail of the cows veered south, he slowed Shadow's pace to a walk and studied the ground over which they passed.

Abruptly he drew rein, turned Shadow's head and rode a straight line to the river, still studying the ground intently. At the water's edge he pulled up, turned and glanced back toward the cliffs.

"Yes, horse, just as I expected," he remarked. "In comparatively recent times, geologically speaking, say a hundred thousand years back, this whole section was highly volcanic, and vestiges of volcanic activity are still apparent in the region. Mt. Capulin, for instance, is the last of the active volcanoes in the southwestern United States. You'll notice those cliffs are curiously striated, a volcanic manifestation."

He paused a moment to roll a cigarette and resumed.

"Yes, there is indubitable evidence that a stream once flowed this way to empty into the river. We just passed over an underlying slab of rock where the little water-washed boulders and pebbles have not been deeply buried under drifting soil. Yes, a stream once flowed here, and a rather large one. Where did it come from? That I hope to learn very shortly."

Turning Shadow's head again, he rode back to where the bristle of tall chaparral grew at the base of the cliffs, edging his mount in close to the outer straggle, and chuckled with satisfaction.

"Yep, here it is," he said. "You'll notice, horse, that for a little stretch of growth the leaves are beginning to shrivel and brown. An old trick, but it works. However, the gents were a bit careless and made one of the little slips the outlaw brand always

113

seems prone to make. Watch, now."

He dismounted, seized one of the stout mesquite trunks and heaved. The trunk came out of the ground quite easily, for the wide spreading of roots had been cut away and the lower end of the trunk sharpened to a stake that was driven into the ground. He set the bush aside, tackled another, and still another.

"Yes, an old trick," he repeated. "But the hellions neglected to change the stands of growth when the leaves began to shrivel."

He straightened up and gazed at that which the removal of the bushes had revealed.

Splitting the face of the cliff was a dark opening, perhaps a score of feet in width by something less than half that in height.

"Yep, there's where the stream emerged from its underground channel," he said. "Now it's up to us to try and find out where it dived into the ground, a common occurrence in this section, before some convulsion of earth cut off the flow."

Nearby was a stand of sotol, prevalent in the region, and dry sotol stalks make excellent torches. He secured several and stowed them in a saddle pouch. Then he led Shadow through the gap in the brush and carefully replaced the removed bushes.

Mounting, he lighted one of the stalks and moved his horse into the cave.

The roof of the bore, he noted, was cracked and fissured, but the walls had been worn smooth by the action of the water. The floor was also smooth except for a littering of small boulders and pebbles, and had a very slight upward slant. It was rather a tight squeeze, but by bending forward he was able to keep from brushing the crown of his hat against the roof.

Shadow's hoofbeats echoed hollowly from the rock walls, but he encountered no difficulty aside from skating over a loose boulder now and then, to the accompaniment of disgusted snorts.

Slade noted that the cave trended steadily west by south, with an occasional shallow curve. On and on it stretched through the black dark illumined only by the flickering glow of the torch. But to all appearances there were no pitfalls which El Halcón deemed was to be expected.

Shadow trudged along steadily, at a slow pace. Slade lighted another torch, and still another, the bore being longer than he had calculated it would be.

Abruptly the tunnel widened. Slade pulled his mount to a halt and held the torch high.

"Here's where they hold the cows during

the daylight hours," he told Shadow. "Has the look of a hole-up too."

There was indeed evidence of human occupancy. Several rude bunks were built along the walls. There was a stack of staple provision, some bundles of hay. Beside fire-blackened stones were cooking utensils.

All of which was interesting and might be put to use. With a final glance around, he rode on, confident he was near the upper mouth of the cave.

Which indeed proved to be the case. The upward slope increased a little, the bore narrowed again, very much, and straightened. Another moment and he saw a greenish glow ahead. A few more of Shadow's long strides and he reached the end of the natural tunnel.

Directly in front of the opening was a stand of tall growth. And he quickly saw that the same method of concealment as featured the Valley mouth of the bore had been employed here.

Dismounting, he removed a couple of the stake-end bushes and set them aside. Very cautiously he peered out. In every direction stretched the deserted level prairie. And not too far ahead was the scanty foliage that edged the desert on the south, with the loom of the hills beyond. A drive that could be negotiated by a herd in the hours of darkness. He glanced back at the cavern mouth.

"The man who discovered that hole, recognized its possibilities and put them to use has more than a smattering of geological knowledge," he remarked to Shadow. "Jeff Meader? He wouldn't recognize geology if he met it in the middle of the road! No, the gent who calls himself Muerto is a much smarter and better educated man. And I've a feeling that he'll make one more little slip that will give him away. Well, we'll see."

He paused for a last glance at the cave, noticing that the overhang at its mouth was splintered and broken, the roof cracks continuing for several feet into the bore.

"Wouldn't take much of a shock to bring it down," he observed. "But I reckon it will hold unless a lightning bolt or a slight earthquake comes along. Evidently has been in that condition for quite a while. We won't bother our heads about it unless we happen to be beneath it when and if it takes a notion to let go."

He led his mount into the open and carefully replaced the camouflaging bushes. He was confident he had left nothing behind to betray his passage through the cave. The burned-out sockets of the sotol torches he had stowed in his saddle pouch, to discard later.

It had taken much longer to cross and recross the valley, reveal the bore and pass through it than he had anticipated, and the sun was on the slant of the western sky.

Sitting on his tall black horse, a striking figure against the declining sun's glow, he gazed at the table of beauty set in banquet for the eyes of the beholder. East and south stretched the amber waves of the rangeland. The mountain crests deepened in purple as the saffron loosened in the west, and a gossamer cloud of Tyrian dye floated over distant Tucumcari. A grand land, well worth fighting for! He spoke to Shadow and rode toward Amarillo, where the pulsing stream of life flaunted its own turbulent beauty.

It was long past dark when he reached the Cowboy Capital, to find it apparently recovered from the effects of the payday bust and going strong. He stabled and cared for his horse and repaired to the sheriff's office, where Carter was anxiously awaiting his arrival.

"Well, did you learn anything?" the sheriff asked.

"All I needed to," Slade replied, and rendered a brief account of his discovery.

"And you figured it all out in advance!" Carter exclaimed admiringly.

"Well, when it was evident those stolen cows didn't go up the cliffs, it was fairly logical to reason that they must have somehow gone through them, so I worked on that premise."

"And you figure the water bored that hole through the cliffs?"

"Possibly. Then again, in the beginning it may have been blasted through by some terrific outburst of steam in the course of a volcanic eruption. Then somehow the stream got diverted into it for a period, say a hundred thousand years or so, until the flow was cut off by another eruption, or possibly by an earthquake. Such things have occurred in many parts of the world. Anyhow, there it is, providing a perfect set-up for a widelooper smart enough to discover it and put it to use. A hundred persons could have passed that way and never noticed anything out of the ordinary."

"But not one El Halcón," the sheriff observed dryly. "Well, now you've found it, what are we going to do with it?"

"Try and put it to a good use," Slade replied. "Get in touch with Keith Norman and John Fletcher and Jeff Meader. Tell them if they lose cattle some night to let us know about it right away. Then we may be able to set a trap for the devils. If they do grab off a herd, they'll hole it up during the daylight hours, which should give us time to get there before they move on with the coming of darkness."

"By gosh! That sounds real," applauded Carter. "Should be easy as fallin' off a slick log in the water."

"Sounds a mite too easy, and I get suspicious of anything that sounds easy," Slade said. "Got to catch your rabbit 'fore you cook it, and we've got to get our wideloop-ing *amigos* on the move before we'll have a chance to twirl our loop. Well, we'll see."

"And now how about the Trail End and a surrounding?" the sheriff suggested. "Imagine it's been quite a while since you ate."

"Nothing since before daybreak," Slade admitted. "Let's go."

"By the way," Carter remarked as they set out, "Watson Gaynard is settin' up his drilling rig over beyond the lake. Building a derrick and getting the machinery in place. Imagine you'll want to look it over."

"Yes, I will," Slade replied, his eyes thoughtful.

The Trail End was busy, per usual. Swivel-eye came over to greet them and then hurried to the kitchen.

"Doc Beard gave Meader a once-over and told him there was nothing to worry about," the sheriff observed. "Prescribed a shot of redeye with another as a chaser."

"Doc's favorite prescription," Slade smiled. "Seems to work."

Carter meditatively studied his glass, took a sip, downed the rest at a swallow and hammered for a refill.

"And you really figure we should be able to knock off the devils there by that hole in the ground?" he asked.

"I don't see any reason why we shouldn't," Slade answered. "The terrain is made to order for us. The cave mouth is at the base of a low ridge heavily brush-grown to provide plenty of cover. They'd be bunched behind the herd coming out and at a disadvantage. Yes, we should be able to bag the whole crowd.

"That is," he added with a smile, "if they'll cooperate and run off a few cows at just the right time."

"If past performance counts for anything, they will," growled Carter. "They've sure been running 'em high, wide and handsome of late."

The sheriff did not exaggerate. Rustling was the bane of the Panhandle during the period. It was estimated that the loss of stock to the Comancheros and the outlaws who came after them ran to around three hundred thousand head.

They ate a leisurely and relaxing dinner, with coffee for El Halcón and another snort for the sheriff with which to wash it down. Then Slade announced, "I'm going to bed. Those rocks I slept on for a while this morning weren't overly soft. A mattress for a change will be a welcome relief."

"Okay," said Carter. "See you sometime tomorrow."

TWELVE

The following afternoon, Slade walked to where Watson Gaynard was setting up his drilling rig. The site was a bustle of activity. The tall derrick was already rising, the massive supporting vertical beams slanting slightly inward, the transverse timbers securely bolted to them. The boiler and the engine were ready to go in place.

The workers were quiet, capable-appearing men. They slanted glances toward the Ranger, but did not speak. Slade instantly noted an article of apparel affected by one, which held his attention. However, he proffered no comment.

Gaynard was busy directing, ordering,

advising. He at once joined El Halcón, smiling and nodding.

"So you made it!" he exclaimed heartily. "Glad you did; we're just getting under way. I'll explain things as we walk around."

He gestured to the beginning of the derrick. "Twenty feet square at the base, with a seventy-five-foot height. I figure that should do it," he said.

"Although we may have to go pretty deep," he added. "Wait just a minute, I'm needed over there."

He approached the derrick, gave some instructions to a man working there, who looked uncertain, asked a question, which Gaynard answered. The man nodded and went back to work. Gaynard returned to the Ranger to say:

"Have to keep a pretty close watch on things or mistakes will be made. My boys are good workers, but, after all, that's just what they are, workers, and accustomed to someone else doing the thinking. Doubtless you have observed it in your line of business."

"It is sometimes quite obvious," Slade agreed. Gaynard apparently did not notice that the answer was decidedly noncommittal.

They walked around together for a while,

Gaynard explaining, the Ranger listening. Finally Slade thanked him for his courtesy, promised to return soon for another look at the project, and made his way slowly to the sheriff's office, deep in thought.

"The little slips," he murmured to himself, "always they make them. The one today is number four, I'd say. The loose threads are tightening, weaving into a pattern, but still nothing definite to go on. Well, the next one, if there is a next one, may provide opportunity. Here's hoping."

When he arrived at the office, Sheriff Carter supplied him with a cup of coffee and looked expectant.

"How'd you make out?" he asked.

"Well," Slade replied, sipping the coffee, "today I saw something I never saw before, and never expected to see."

"Yes?" Carter prompted.

"Today I saw a drilling rig erector wearing rangeland riding boots on the job."

"Rangeland riding boots?" the sheriff repeated interrogatively.

"Yes, cowhand boots instead of the brogans usually worn by that type of worker."

"Is there anything you don't notice!" sighed Carter. "What does it mean?"

"Could mean nothing, and then again it could mean a good deal," Slade replied.

"What else?" the sheriff asked.

"Gaynard has four men working under him," Slade answered reflectively. "A couple of them know something about the work, not too much, but something. I'd say they were probably employed as laborers, one time or another, on a drilling project. The other two know practically nothing about such work. Gaynard has to direct every move they make, instruct them what to do and how to do it."

"Maybe that sort was the best he could tie onto," hazarded the sheriff.

"That could be an explanation," Slade admitted. "One nobody would be liable to contradict. I would very likely accept it myself, were there nothing else to be considered."

"What else?" the very interested sheriff wanted to know.

"In the first place," Slade explained, "he couldn't possibly drill to the depth he told the interested businessmen he intends to. His tower derrick is not tall enough, and he hasn't enough power. He'll get water, all right, but not the pure, deep stream water he promises."

"Where will he get it from?" asked Carter.

"Gaynard," Slade explained, "is thoroughly grounded in the science of geology.

He knows as well as I know that the water he will get will be the underflow from Amarillo Lake. I hope he doesn't realize I know it, and I don't think he does."

"From Amarillo Lake?"

"That's right. It is obvious that more water flows into the Lake than, to all appearances flows out of it. That surplus water must go somewhere. Near the middle of the Lake is a slight swirl and eddy that marks where the water drains to a subterranean channel. It is very slight, but can be seen."

"By your eyes," grunted the sheriff. "Go on."

"The water very likely falls to a considerable depth before reaching its channel, and the lake is deep. Gaynard will have to drill quite a distance to contact the flow, but not nearly as deep as he has led people to believe. And he won't pump out the type of water he has promised, if he gets that far."

"Meaning that he's putting something over on folks, eh?" growled Carter.

"He certainly is," Slade replied, with a slight smile. "Yes, he is thoroughly grounded in geology, as he proved when he discovered that hidden way through the cliffs from the Canadian River Valley."

The sheriff stared wide-eyed. "You — you mean you figure he is Muerto?" sputtered

126

the astounded peace officer.

"He is," Slade said unequivocally. "Watson Gaynard is Muerto or Muerto is Watson Gaynard, take your pick."

Carter gasped and rumbled, gazing at the Ranger as if convinced he had taken leave of his sanity.

"How — how do you figure it?" he finally asked, increduously.

"That first night, when he outlined his plan, about half his talk was gibberish, scientific gibberish," Slade replied.

"I know I couldn't make head or tail of it," the sheriff interpolated.

"Which was just the condition he hoped and expected to prevail," Slade continued. "Expecting that neither could I make anything of it. And when he said he intended to drill close to the lake, I knew there was something phony about the affair. The deep subterranean water of which he spoke so glibly is not there, but farther to the southwest. Right then I began taking considerable interest in *amigo* Gaynard. And when I tracked those stolen cows to the opening in the Valley wall, I no longer had much doubt about him. And I recalled that when the attempts were made against my life, one of which very nearly caused Jeff Meader to get his comeuppance, each time Gaynard was present a short time before, keeping tabs on me and my movements, of course. And no doubt you'll remember remarking on his dusty clothes the night after the cows were widelooped."

"Yep, I do remember noticing that," conceded Carter.

"Well," Slade said, "that dust with which his clothes were sprinkled was desert alkali dust. He could have gotten it no place else but on or near the Tucumcari Desert. Beginning to catch on?"

"Darned if you ain't making out a case, all right," the sheriff admitted.

"The drilling project is a perfect cover-up," Slade resumed. "It explained his frequent rides, and it put him in a position to learn things, like the fact the Tascosa stage was packing money, which it rarely does. I'm of the opinion that very likely he was once, in an engineering capacity, connected with some oil production outfit, perhaps at Beaumont, where he familiarized himself with all the angles of the drilling business. And for some reason, perhaps from having suffered an injustice, he turned to outlawry, which has happened before in more than one instance. A clever, intelligent and able man taking the wrong fork in the trail. Why doesn't really matter. What counts is the indubitable fact that he did."

"All set to drop a loop on him?" Carter asked.

"For what?" Slade countered. "For making dupes of certain trusting business individuals? I could expose him, but I couldn't make the charge stick. He could claim he had just made an honest mistake, and nobody could successfully contradict him. And after all, I am a Texas Ranger, not here to protect businessmen from their own stupidity, but to bring a robber and a killer to justice. As I have pointed out, the water-drilling project is a cover-up. I doubt he intends to finish it, in entirety."

"Meaning that after another good haul or two he may pull out?"

"It is possible," Slade admitted. "When he decides he has about worked the section for all it's worth and has made the really big haul he has in mind, he may move on to fresh pastures, as others have done before him. I hope we'll be able to do something about him before he reaches that decision, for I'd hate to have to chase him all over Texas, perhaps elsewhere."

"If he takes a notion to run some more cows, maybe that'll give us a break, now that you know how he does it," said Carter.

"Yes, that might provide us with opportunity to corral the whole bunch, if we learn about it in time," Slade agreed.

"I sent Norman and Fletcher and Jeff Meader word to let us know right off if they miss some critters," Carter replied. "Figure he might really wideloop a few 'fore long?"

"I consider it possible," Slade said. "Cows are quick and easy money, with usually not much risk attached. He'll need to keep his devils in spending money, and he very likely believes his scheme is foolproof."

"Would be were it not for El Halcón," grunted the sheriff. "You mentioned the slips he made, but not the big one. The big one was not pullin' out the minute he learned you were in the section."

"Nice of you to say it, but I doubt if he really knows a great deal about me, perhaps thinks I'm considerably overrated. In which he may be right, for that matter."

A derisive snort from the sheriff.

"I doubt he has any idea I'm a Ranger and doesn't give overly much thought to a special deputy sheriff. Quite likely figures I've just been lucky enough to get a few breaks; everything that's happened could be interpreted that way."

"He'll know better before you're finished with him," the sheriff predicted confidently.

"Again, nice of you to say it," Slade

130

smiled. "Here's hoping you prove to be a prophet with honor."

"I ain't in the habit of being wrong," retorted Carter. "Especially where you are concerned. By the way, I expect old Keith and Jerry Norman to ride in this evening."

"Hope so," Slade replied. "Jerry is good company."

"Yep," said the sheriff. "Just a penny in size, but she's sound money.

"And you figure the feller wearing the boots is a cowhand?"

"Is or has been," Slade answered. "He's certainly not a rigger; one of the pair that knows nothing about the work." "And I reckon you call that one of the slips the horned toads made."

"That's right. They always seem to make them, sooner or later. Yes, one of the slips."

For some time they sat discussing the matter pro and con, with no very satisfactory results. Looked like there was really nothing to do but wait and see which way the cat would jump; and endeavoring to anticipate feline movements was in the nature of a thankless task.

Finally the sheriff glanced out the window at the flaming glory of the sunset, which Slade had been watching for some time, and knocked ash out of his pipe.

"Suppose we amble over to the Trail End for a small surrounding," he suggested. "All this palaver makes me hungry, and a snort or two won't go bad; thinking and talking is a thirsty business."

"Guess we could do worse," Slade agreed. "We sure don't seem to be getting anywhere here."

The Trail End was busy, although the evening rush had not yet set in. Busy, but fairly quiet. So they enjoyed a leisurely dinner in comfort, topped off with a snort for the sheriff and a final cup of steaming coffee for Slade. After which cigarette and pipe came into play.

"Looks like it might be a quiet night for a change," the sheriff remarked, glancing around.

"Yes, it does look sort of that way," Slade agreed.

"Not that you can ever be sure," Carter added pessimistically. "This blasted town can cut loose riproarin' hell-raisin' from nothing."

A quiet night for Amarillo, perhaps, but something quite different elsewhere, and not too far off.

"I knew it!" Carter suddenly chuckled. "Here they come."

It was indeed old Keith Norman and

Jerry, the rancher looking or pretending to look disgruntled.

"Wouldn't let me have a minute's peace till I agreed to bring her to town," Norman snorted. "The older I get the less I can guess about women and their notions. You'd think she hadn't seen the young hellion for a year, 'stead of just a coupla days or so."

"Time is relative, Uncle Keith," Jerry pointed out as she sat down beside Slade. "If you are sprawled in a comfortable chair in the shade with a drink in front of you, all day seems like a minute, but if you were sitting on a hot stove, a minute would seem a year."

"I heard it told different, but I reckon the idea is the same," old Keith commented dryly.

Jerry giggled, and slanted Slade a glance through her lashes.

"I'm hungry," she announced.

Swivel-eye bustled to the kitchen to care for that lack.

And so the evening wore on, with jest and laughter and good fellowship. It was fortunate for their peace of mind that they could not gaze south a dozen miles or so.

After crossing open rangeland, the trail from Amarillo to Canyon reached a point where southward the country roughened into breaks where the chaparral grew tall. Ahead, slightly to the southeast, rose the grim loom of the Cap Rock.

Canyon was an old cowtown that later would achieve the dignity of a seat of learning — The West Texas Teachers-College due to occupy former lands of the T-Anchor Ranch which, the night Walt Slade and his companions made merry in the Trail End, was still a going concern.

There was no bank at Canyon, but the little town did boast a stage that made the run to Amarillo and return several times a week. Sometimes the stage carried money, not much as a rule, for deposit in the Amarillo bank.

But there were exceptions. Tonight, due to a consummated land deal, there was a hefty passel of *dinero* stashed inside the locked coach.

The night run was also an exception, having been decided on by the management for several reasons. A decision, incidentally, that was not generally known. At least was not supposed to be known.

One of the reasons was the fact that the trail from Canyon to Amarillo was hardly ever ridden at night by characters questionable or otherwise. Another, the unscheduled night run would accommodate no passengers, none being wanted inside that money-packing coach.

However, the management was taking no chances. An armed guard sat beside the driver, who also packed artillery and knew how to use it. And inside the locked coach was another guard, also armed with rifle and six-gun. If gentlemen with share-the-wealth notions made a try for the stage, they would meet with a hot reception.

Furthermore, the terrain was not favorably adapted to a hold-up. Although brush encroached on stretches of the trail, it was generally not thick enough to provide adequate concealment for a robber band.

So it appeared there was little to worry about.

The sky was brilliant with stars, and there was a low moon. Which was also to the advantage of the stage crew. The driver and the guards, while keeping a sharp watch, talked and joked as the coach, drawn by four sturdy horses, rolled on through the breaks with the scatterings of brush on either side.

Without an instant's warning, a streak of fire ran across the trail directly in front. A wall of flame roared up. The terrified horses bucked, reared, slewed sideways and around. The coach rocked, lurched, slammed into a stout trunk at the edge of the track and didn't quite turn over as the horses tore free and fled back the way they had come, screaming their fear of the horror that had leaped before their eyes.

The driver, the reins whisked from his hands, was hurled off balance. The guard was thrown from the seat and against the dashboard. From inside the coach came a yell of pain.

And in the straggle of brush to the left, five prone figures leaped erect, guns blazing.

The driver and the outside guard, both wounded by that booming volley, tried valiantly to fight back. But both were completely off balance, half stunned by the demoralizing unexpectedness of the onslaught. The driver fell from the seat to the ground, to lie motionless. Another instant and the dead outside guard lay beside him.

The inside guard was shooting through the little barred window. Answering bullets thudded against the wooden side of the couch; but he continued to fire.

A louder report, the heavy clang of a rifle! Again, and yet again, and there were no more slugs from inside the coach.

From the brush swarmed five masked men. A bullet smashed the lock, the door was jerked open. Callously shoving the still form of the guard aside, one of the bandits seized the plump money pouch. They leaped over the smolders of the fire, ran up the trail a short distance, dived into the brush. Another moment and a beat of fast hoofs faded into the north.

And from the dust of the trail, glazed, unseeing eyes glared up at the splendor of the star-strewn sky.

THIRTEEN

A T-Anchor cowhand, riding home from Amarillo, came upon the scene of horror and death. He made sure the driver and the guards were beyond human help, paid no attention to anything else, and sent his horse racing back to Amarillo, recalling he had seen Sheriff Carter and his special deputy in the Trail End.

Slade and the others were getting ready to call it a night when the cowhand rushed in and gabbled forth the story of what he saw.

"Didn't happen in my bailiwick, that's Randal County," said the sheriff, adding, with a meaningful glance at the Ranger, in whose "bailiwick" it most assuredly was, "but I reckon we'd better ride down there."

"Yes, I guess we'd better," Slade replied.

"Just a minute, though."

He gestured the still highly excited cowboy to a chair, ordered him a drink.

"You are sure the driver and the guards were dead?" he asked.

"No doubt about it," answered the puncher, gulping his drink, Slade motioning a refill. "Driver and outside guard were shot to pieces. Inside guard had a bullet hole between his eyes, a big one, looked like it was made by a rifle slug."

The impact of the alcohol had a steadying effect and the cowhand grew calmer.

"The coach was jammed against the brush, almost into it," he explained in answer to Slade's question as to what he saw. "Horses had busted the harness and were gone. Seemed to me I smelled something burning. I was sorta worked up and didn't pay much attention to anything except those three poor devils."

"I see," Slade said. "Take it easy and put away your snort. There is evidently no hurry.

"You stay here until we tie onto our horses and a lantern," he added. "Will give your cayuse a chance to rest a little." He turned to Jerry.

"See you later," he told her. She shook her head and sighed resignedly.

"I'll look after her," Norman promised.

"Be looking for you, son."

"Just a routine chore of checking, nothing to worry about," Slade said, patting her hand.

"I hope so," she replied. Her anxious eyes followed his progress to the swinging doors as he and the sheriff headed for the stable.

"Figure it was Muerto and his bunch?" the sheriff asked as they cinched up and the stable keeper scurried to fetch a lantern.

"Of course," El Halcón answered. "Has all the earmarks of his fine hand. And I guarantee we will find something highly ingenious and original. Yes, it was our *amigo* Watson Gaynard who engineered the deal. Sort of explains, too, why one of his rig workers was wearing riding boots, figuring on doing a little riding later on and made the slip of donning his boots before coming to work on the rig. We'll see."

In deference to the cowhand's tired horse, Slade set a moderate pace and the false dawn had fled ghost-like across the sky by the time they reached the scene of the outrage. Slade at once went to work reconstructing the crime.

What caught his attention immediately was a dark streak that ran across the narrow trail from side to side a short distance ahead of where stood the stalled coach. He picked up a handful of the substance, sniffed it, and whistled under his breath.

"Didn't I tell you we'd discover something out of the ordinary?" he said to Carter. "Of all the devilish tricks!"

"What in blazes is it?" demanded the sheriff, peering close at what Slade held in his hand.

"This," Slade explained, "is charred cotton waste that had been drenched with kerosene. The hellion dug a narrow and shallow trench across the trail and packed it with the oil-soaked waste. As the stage approached, a match was touched to the waste. It flared up in a sheet of flame right under the lead horses' noses. Scared the daylights out of them. They whirled around trying to escape the fire, tore loose and slammed the coach into the growth, throwing the driver and the guards off balance. The devils mowed them down from the brush. Let's try and find how they managed to keep out of sight in this thin growth."

He entered the chaparral opposite the coach, held the lantern low and carefully scanned the ground.

"Just as I thought," he announced. "They lay down, hidden by the tall grass that grows at the edge of the trail, and waited until the stage was wrecked, then went to work and murdered the driver and outside guard. Now let's see."

Moving to the coach, he examined the near side and nodded.

"Peppered with six-gun slugs that didn't quite penetrate the thick wood," he said. "Evidently the inside guard fought back. Then somebody, very likely Muerto himself, went to work with a rifle and killed the guard. Well, I guess that's all. We will leave everything as is; I desire the sheriff of Randal County, and the stage people, to view the situation as it stands. Now we'd better head for Canyon and report. Just a minute, though. I imagine the devils tethered their horses a little ways farther up the trail until they were ready to hightail after tying onto the money."

Which investigation proved to be the case.

The East was flushing scarlet and rose as they mounted and headed for Canyon. Not far down the trail they found the stage horses, recovered from their fright and trying to graze. They were freed of the broken harness and left where they were.

"The stage people will have to send a crew to repair the coach — I noticed one front wheel is splintered — and they'll pick up the cayuses," Slade said. "Okay, let's go."

It was well past daybreak when they

reached Canyon, and folks were already astir. The cowhand, thoroughly familiar with the town, located the stage manager, who, as was to be expected, was greatly disturbed.

"Yes, the devils made a good haul, more than fifteen thousand dollars," he told Slade. "Hits us rather hard. We are insured, of course, but I expect it will skyrocket our rates. However, the money doesn't matter so much — that can always be made back — but those poor men who were foully murdered. There is no bringing them back. Good men, all of them. Been with me for years."

When he discussed the money loss the manager's face, while concerned, which was not unnatural, had been composed enough. But as he spoke of the murdered driver and guards, his face was drawn, haggard, a tortured look in his eyes. Slade felt sympathy, and respect, for him.

"There is one event unto all," he said gently. "Sooner or later we all must face it, and very likely it is not terrible. They are at peace."

"Thank you," replied the manager. "That makes me feel better. You have a wonderful understanding, Mr. Slade."

While awaiting the appearance of Tol Prouty, the Randal County sheriff, well known to Brian Carter, Slade and the latter repaired to a nearby restaurant pointed out by the stage manager and partook of coffee and a snack. They had just finished eating when Prouty arrived and the robbery and killings were discussed.

"Appears there were no witnesses, and Bert, the cowhand, discovered the bodies," Prouty remarked. "Guess an inquest would be but a formality and hold that the driver and the guards met their deaths at the hands of parties unknown."

"Looks that way," Carter agreed, "but do as you please about it. Guess there's no sense in Slade and me attending if you do decide to hold an inquest?"

"Don't see how you could do any good," Prouty conceded.

A little later, a wagon containing tools, fresh harness, and a repair crew rolled north. On the return trip it would fetch the bodies to Canyon.

Slade and Carter accompanied it, along with Sheriff Prouty, and paused long enough at the scene of the robbery to point out salient features of Slade's findings for the benefit of the Randal County peace officer. After which they said goodbye to Prouty and continued to Amarillo.

It was well past midmorning when they

reached the Cowboy Capital, but in the Trail End, sitting at a table, was a very weary and lonely-looking little feminine figure.

"I just couldn't sleep until I knew for sure you were back safe," she told Slade. "Now I will."

The sheriff smiled.

FOURTEEN

Sunset was fading when Slade and the sheriff sat in the latter's office and talked over matters.

"The hellion put one across, all right," Carter observed.

"He certainly did," Slade replied. "And the method he employed was unique, to put it mildly. He's something to reckon with."

"Figure he'll lay off for a while, now that he's well heeled?" wondered Carter.

"I doubt it," Slade said. "He is not the sort to remain idle for long, and although he made a good haul last night, it isn't so much when divided among seven or eight, which very likely his bunch numbers, perhaps more. Well, here's hoping next he'll make a try for some cows. That could give us a break, for I'm still of the opinion that he has no idea his way out of the Valley has

144

been discovered. Yes, it could give us a break."

"Uh-huh, that is if you don't *make* a break first," said Carter.

"I fear you expect too much of me," Slade laughed.

"Not when based on past performance," the sheriff declared sturdily.

A period of silence followed, while outside the dusk deepened to violet shot with golden gleams as an old Mexican with a short ladder and an oil torch lighted the street lamps.

"By the way, almost forgot," said the sheriff. "As you suggested, I told Grumley to keep an eye on that well rig. A little while before you showed up he dropped in and said Gaynard was there this afternoon but had only two men working on the derrick. Wonder what became of the other two?"

"Hard to tell," Slade replied thoughtfully. "Probably scouting something preparatory to another raid. Chances are we'll learn, and not enjoy the learning."

Carter growled a cuss word or two and glanced at the clock.

"Had your breakfast yet?" he asked. Slade shook his head.

"Waited to eat with you," he answered. "Jerry should be showing up soon, too."

"Then suppose we amble over to the Trail End and grab off a bite," suggested the sheriff. "I waited to eat with *you*, and right now I'm beginning to feel a mite lank. Been quite a while since we had that snack down at Canyon."

Slade was amenable to the suggestion and they set out, to find a hungry and impatient Jerry awaiting them at the Trail End.

"It's about time!" she scolded. "A girl could starve to death waiting for you slow pokes to show up. Thank goodness there goes Mr. Sanders to tell the cook to rattle his hocks."

The night passed peacefully. Jerry and Slade visited the Washout but did not remain long, for old Keith desired to get an early start home the following day.

"Stay away too long and some blankety-blank is liable to steal the roof over my head," he declared.

Several quiet days followed. That is, quiet so far as outlaw depredations were concerned. Amarillo was its usual turbulent self, and anything but quiet.

Beside the lake, Watson Gaynard's derrick was rising, but Slade did not visit the site, being in no mood for talking with the cold killer, and failing to see how any advantage

146

could accrue from intercourse with him.

"The less attention we appear to pay the hellion the better," he told Carter. "May lull him into a sense of false security, and avoids the risk of making a slip that might put him on his guard."

"You ain't in the habit of making slips, but I reckon you're right," conceded the sheriff. "And keeping my face straight when the sidewinder is around strains my insides. Oh, well, as the Devil drives! as the saying has it. Guess again we'll just have to wait."

"About the size of it," Slade agreed.

But as the days passed with nothing happening, he grew increasingly restless and uneasy. That Muerto would strike again and soon, he was convinced. And were he unable to anticipate what the shrewd devil had in mind, he greatly feared it would be attended by another killing or two. Gaynard's policy appeared to be one of leaving no witnesses. And Slade believed that along with other unpleasant attributes, he was very probably afflicted with the blood lust. Certainly looked that way. Not beyond the realm of possibility that a grave injustice or a bitter wrong had caused him to take the wrong fork in the trail, and Slade's experience had been that an able and intelligent man brooding over such gradually developed a hatred for all humanity and vented his spleen on anyone he happened to have at his mercy. Thus glutting a vicarious revenge.

The West had known many such examples — John Wesley Hardin, Billy the Kid, Doc Holliday, to mention but a few. Slade believed Watson Gaynard might well fall into that category.

Which was not calculated to enhance the peace of mind of a law enforcement officer opposed to such a character.

After three days devoid of activity, El Halcón could stand it no longer.

"I think I'll take a ride," he told Carter. "I'm gradually going loco, sitting around doing nothing. Figure it might be a good notion to amble over to the Valley and find out if old Estaban has learned anything that could prove of value. May pay a visit to the Quijanos, Rafael and Rosa; I promised them I would."

"Okay," replied the sheriff, "but keep your eyes open. Can expect anything from that horned toad."

Slade promised to do so, cinched up and rode north. Shadow, tired as his master of being cooped up, snorted agreement to the idea and stepped out briskly, Slade allowing him to choose his own gait, which was plenty fast.

Slade gave but cursory thought to the sheriff's warning. Nobody could follow him and not be spotted by El Halcón's eyes. And certainly nobody knew he intended riding out of town; he didn't know it himself five minutes prior to his decision to do so.

Therefore, although he was automatically watchful as a matter of habit, he paid little attention to his surroundings and gave himself over to the enjoyment of the ride through the beauties of the day.

The low-lying sun cast a mantle of red-gold over the rangeland. Quail whistled. High in the blue of the sky a lark sang. As he neared the Valley, he could see Tucumcari Peak, its towering crest ringed with saffron flame, its mighty chest and shoulders swathed in royal purple. The restless and ofttimes futile striving of mankind, the venom of hate, and the bitter broth of vengeance seemed very far away.

Sunshine and peace! The sweet, restful peace of drowsing nature.

Or so it seemed.

With the sun dropping behind the rim of the horizon, Slade negotiated the descent without mishap and rode steadily up the Valley until he reached Estaban's cabin, where he received a warm welcome. Once again Shadow shared quarters with Carmencita, the pensive mule, while their masters sat down to an appetizing repast.

After they finished eating, they talked together for some time, Slade recounting his recent adventures, Estaban clucking in his throat and wagging his white head as the tale progressed.

"What a life of violence *Capitán* leads!" he said when El Halcón paused. "In the air he breathes, peril is. But in the shadow of the hand of *El Dios* he walks, so no harm can befall him."

"Gracias!" Slade replied soberly. "I like to think it so."

Estaban didn't have much to tell him, but what he did have caused the Ranger's brows to draw together thoughtfully.

"Twice strange men rode up the Valley," he said. "Here they did not pause, nor at the Quijanos' cabin, nor at the plazas farther on, but rode steadily westward, as if some rendezvous they had."

"Quite likely they did have," Slade commented. "How are the Quijaños?"

"Excellent health they enjoy," Estaban replied. "Nobody has them molested, and yesterday those who have been keeping watch withdrew, having gardens and flocks of their own to tend."

"I think I'll ride up there for a word with them," Slade said.

"Pleased greatly they will be to see *Capitán,*" Estaban predicted. "Will you here return tonight?"

"Wouldn't be surprised," Slade replied. "I may take a notion to ride on up the Valley, but more likely I'll come back and spend the night with you.

"In a way I'm playing a hunch," he added.

"A hunch?"

"A premonition that something is not just right," Slade explained. "Perhaps because of your mention of strange men riding up the Valley. I know it sounds loco, but it is something I've learned from experience not to disregard."

"Really, it sounds not so loco to me," said Estaban. "Sound reasoning one might say. Which I think are in reality *Capitán's* hunches, as he calls them. *Vaya usted con Dios!*"

Getting the rig on Shadow, who appeared full of oats and in a complacent frame of mind, Slade sent him ambling up the Valley through the silvery sheen of the moonlight that made each twig and leaf a jewel.

Again Slade let him set the pace, which this time was not overly fast, in deference perhaps to the bounteous helping of oats he had absorbed.

After they covered several miles, however, the cayuse began picking up speed. Now they were not far from the Quijano cabin — in fact the clearing in which it stood was around the next bend and only a few hundred yards distant.

Suddenly Slade jerked erect from his easy lounge in the saddle. Directly ahead sounded a crackle of gunfire, the spiteful, whiplash reports of six-guns, punctuated by the heavy boom of a Sharpes fifty-caliber.

Slade's voice rang out, "Trail, Shadow, trail!"

Instantly the great black lunged forward, his hoofs spurning the earth, and in three strides was going full speed. He rounded the bend to the clearing on which the Quijano cabin sat and into the middle of action a-plenty.

Crouched in the brush diagonally from its door, three men were shooting at the cabin. Intermittent booms sounded inside the building. And as Shadow skated to a halt, a flaming torch soared through the air to land on the cabin roof. Instantly the tinder-dry thatch caught and began burning briskly.

At the sound of Shadow's irons, the three gunmen slewed around and Slade felt the air of passing slugs. He whipped out both

152

Colts and, weaving, ducking in the saddle, answered the outlaws shot for shot.

One lurched forward, sagged, fell to the ground to lie motionless. Another gave a yelp of pain. Then, both remaining on their feet, they dived into the brush, crashed through it. Another instant and a beat of fast hoofs faded up the Valley.

Slade started to send Shadow racing after them, then desisted. Quick work was necessary were the burning cabin to be saved.

"Rafael!" he roared. "Water! Fetch water!"

The door banged open and Rafael appeared, bearing a large bucket, Rosa crowding behind him with another. Slade sidled the disgusted Shadow alongside the front of the cabin and stood in the saddle. Rafael handed up the bucket and Slade doused its contents on the flames. Rosa's bucket followed, Rafael speeding to the spring behind the cabin to refill the one he bore.

For minutes it was touch and go, but repeated dousings finally brought the fire under control. A few more buckets extinguished the last smolders. Slade applied a final drenching, dropping the bucket and leaped lightly to the ground, flashing his white smile at the Mexican pair.

"Never a dull moment around here," he chuckled.

"Capitán!" exclaimed Rafael. "Again you were just in time! Praise *El Dios* for his mercies!"

With a glad little cry, Rosa stood on tiptoes, threw her arms around his neck and kissed him.

"Just what took place here?" Slade asked, patting her shoulder.

"This evening I was most watchful," Rafael explained. "I peered and I listened, for yesterday evening, three men rode past. They rode slowly and appeared to be searching the chaparral with their eyes."

"And yesterday the *amigos* who have been guarding you departed, did they not?" Slade interpolated. "The cunning and patient devils have been waiting all this time to wreak vengeance on you. Go ahead with your yarn."

"And this evening, just a short time back, I heard horses' hoofs approaching slowly," Rafael resumed. "They ceased to beat, and watching from the window, I saw those three *ladrones* stealing forward. I fired my *escopeta,* and missed, for the light was not good. They darted back into the chaparral and began shooting at the window. Even as *Capitán* appeared, they threw the lighted torch. The rest *Capitán* knows."

"Yes," Slade said, "and I feel safe in

predicting you won't be bothered again. The devils will very probably figure it is too risky a business — one wounded and one done for tonight. Fetch a lantern and let's see what we bagged."

The dead outlaw, a blue hole between his glazing eyes, proved to be an unsavory-looking specimen with nothing outstanding about him, so far as Slade could ascertain. His pockets disclosed nothing of significance save quite a sum of money, which Slade passed to Rosa.

"Will pay for your roof," he explained, glancing up at the charred thatch, "and enough left over to buy some ribbons for the next fiesta!"

"For fiestas, a year," Rosa replied, smiling and dimpling.

"I imagine his horse is right where he left it," Slade remarked. "We'll see."

His surmise proved correct; they found the animal, tethered to a branch. Rafael stripped off the rig and put the cayuse in his corral.

"Sheriff can use it to pack the body to town," Slade said. "Leave everything else as is for the sheriff to look over. Now I'll have a cup of coffee with you and then I'm heading for Amarillo to notify Carter of what took place."

As Rosa hurried to prepare the coffee, Rafael asked, "How did *Capitán* come to arrive at so opportune a moment?"

"As I mentioned to Estaban, I sort of played a hunch," Slade answered. "Just had a feeling something was not right. Guess it was a straight one."

"Thanks to the Virgin for *Capitán's* hunches," Rafael said piously.

A little later, Slade said good night to the Quijanos and rode down the Valley, pondering the incident, which he believed might prove of importance. It would at least shake the confidence of the outlaws, his most unexpected appearance. Probably they would conclude that somehow he learned what they had in mind and had taken steps to frustrate it. They could hardly be expected to know that chance had played a large part. Which could be all to the good, from El Halcón's point of view.

He paused at Estaban's cabin to acquaint him with what had taken place, much to the old Mexican's astonishment.

"But, as always, El Halcón was there," was his comment. "And where El Halcón is, evil cannot bide."

FIFTEEN

It was well past midnight when Slade reached Amarillo, but, as he expected, Carter was awaiting him in the Trail End.

He listened with absorbed interest to Slade's account of the attack on the Quijanos.

"Wonder if the hellions sorta figured to take a backhanded slap at you that way?" he observed shrewdly.

"It is possible," Slade conceded. "But if they had such in mind, it backfired a mite."

"Yep, it sure did," the sheriff concurred. "Guess they are beginning to realize plumb for certain what it means to be up against El Halcón. And you're thinning 'em out, you're thinning 'em out."

"But the head of the outfit is still very much on the loose," Slade reminded. "And until we corral him, we can expect more trouble. Yes, you could be right in your surmise relative to the raid on the Quijanos, but then again it may have been but an example of pure viciousness, such as I'm inclined to believe is to be expected from Gaynard."

"Yep, a hyderphobia skunk for fair, with apologies to the real skunk. Well, we'll amble over there after a session of ear pounding and fetch in the carcass. Didn't happen to see him before, say working on that rig?"

"No, he wasn't one of those four," Slade replied. "I don't recall seeing him anywhere."

"Maybe somebody will remember something about him when we put him on exhibition," Carter said hopefully. "Trouble is nobody ever seems to remember anything about the hellions that might do us some good. Oh, well, what was that you once said about time that busts up the rocks giving us the lowdown on everything? Reckon it will all work out, sooner or later."

"And before some other innocent person is murdered, I hope," Slade remarked morosely. "Just pure luck that the Quijanos weren't the victims tonight."

"I got another name for it," differed the sheriff. "Fast and accurate thinking on your part. The minute old Estaban told you about those strange jiggers riding up the Valley, you were on the alert, were you not?"

"Well, it did start me wondering a bit, and curious," Slade admitted.

"Uh-huh, and so you sashayed right off to find out what was in the wind. Anybody else wouldn't have given it a passing thought."

Slade laughed, and didn't argue.

"Suppose we call it a night?" Carter suggested. "I'd like to get started after that carcass before noon; be plenty late getting back as is."

"A notion," Slade agreed. "Let's go."

An hour before noon, Slade and the sheriff set out, riding north by slightly west. But some five miles out of town, El Halcón drew rein, scanned the prairie in every direction, then turned Shadow's nose due east.

"Hey! What does this mean?" demanded the surprised sheriff.

"It means," Slade replied, "that we're heading for another descent I know five miles or so to the east. We are not riding across the open range to the one I almost always use when riding from Amarillo."

"You figure some of those devils might be holed up waiting for us?" asked Carter.

"I don't figure anything for sure, but it is practically certain that Gaynard has long before now learned of what happened in the Valley last night, and it wouldn't require outstanding perspicacity to deduce that we would ride to fetch the body. And as I've said over and over, I don't put anything past him; he seldom misses a trick. He may well have decided that there's an opportunity in the making to get rid of us.

"So we're riding up the Valley from the

east to that western descent, and if there's somebody on the crest waiting for us to put in an appearance, I'll find out. May seem a needless precaution, but it's best not to take unnecessary chances."

"You're darn right," growled Carter. "And thank Pete you don't miss any tricks either. I wouldn't have thought of it and figured it out that way."

The descent to the east was difficult, but the sure-footed horses negotiated it without mishap. Slade set a fast pace up the Valley for several miles, then slowed down, scanning the terrain ahead in every direction, slowed still more. The last quarter of a mile the horses traveled at little better than a walk.

"I'm fairly convinced there's nobody down here," he said instinctively lowering his voice, "but I want to be sure."

A bit farther, Slade veered slightly to the right until he had a fairly good view of the brush crowned crest of the wall. They were close to the descent when he drew rein.

"Here we'll leave the horses," he said. "Can't risk their clumping any further. Okay, stay under cover as much as possible. This may be perfectly silly, but better to be safe than sorry."

Carter nodded vigorous assent and they

stole on until they were almost to where the semblance of a trail wound down from the crest. Here Slade called a halt and stood gazing upward, his eyes narrowing.

"Brian," he whispered, "there's somebody up there, all right."

"How do you know?" the sheriff whispered back.

"Look at the birds fluttering over that thicket to the right of the trail," Slade replied. "Notice how they dive down, sweep up, dive down again, sweep up again. Never settling. Something has them excited and nervous."

"Couldn't it be maybe a coyote or some other critter?" guessed Carter. Slade shook his head.

"A coyote they would understand and pay no mind to," Slade said. "There's something below their perches they don't understand and fear, something beyond their experience. I've a very good notion what that is, having watched their reactions under similar circumstances. Yes, the devils are up there, on that I'll wager."

For several more moments he watched the wheeling birds. More than once little creatures of the wild, good friends to those who understand them and their ways, had saved him from disaster.

"We'll slide up the trail a ways, carefully, then slip into the brush," he told his companion. "That way we should be able to take the hellions in the rear, for they will be watching the prairie. All set? Okay, let's go, and be quiet. Try to step where I step, and no hurrying. One slip will very likely be our last."

Slowly, cautiously, ready for instant action, they mounted the trail. Slade's ears could catch the twittering of the alarmed birds, the sources of the sound remaining stationary, indicating that the drygulchers, were they really there, were not moving about. Which he considered to an extent reassuring.

For the first two-thirds of the way the trail was somewhat winding, but for the last third it straightened out and ran straight to the crest. Slade nodded to the sheriff and they eased into the growth, against the chance that one of the killers might glance down the track. His caution redoubled. Each forward reaching foot tested the ground before he put his weight on it, Carter treading in his steps.

The slow stalk up the steep slope seemed interminable, although the distance was really quite short. From time to time they paused to peer and listen, probing the growth ahead with their gaze, experiencing the unpleasant feeling that watchful eyes might be regarding their approach, fingers tightening on triggers, just waiting until they were within pointblank range with no chance of a miss, with the tearing impact of a bullet the first intimation that they had been spotted.

And then Slade heard, undertoning the chirping of the birds, that which justified his hunch and was definitely reassuring — a low grumble of voices. The drygluchers were there and apparently not aware that they were the hunted instead of the complacent hunters. He slowed the pace still more and they advanced at a rate that would have drawn sneers from an able-bodied snail.

Suddenly there was an excited exclamation directly ahead, followed by another. Slade crouched low, hands streaking to his guns. Spotted!

But nothing happened, although Slade was convinced that something out of the ordinary was in the making. A tense moment and he surged erect, took a long step, another, the sheriff keeping pace. The growth thinned, and he saw the drygulchers.

They were standing in the final fringe of the brush, two of them, each with a rifle clamped to his shoulder, eyes glancing along the sights.

And just rounding a thicket a few hundred yards out on the prairie was a tall man mounted on a big dark horse. And toward his advancing form pointed the two rifle barrels. It was murder that was in the making! And not a second to waste were the horseman's life to be saved. Slade's great voice rolled in thunder —

"Up! You're covered! In the name of the State of Texas!"

The drygulchers whirled, rifles jutting forward. "It's him!" one yelled.

It was the last thing he said on this earth, for even as his rifle flamed, Slade's bullet laced through his heart.

A gasping grunt beside him told Slade the sheriff was hit. But the rugged old peace officer was blazing away as fast as he could squeeze trigger. The second outlaw fell, sprawled motionless beside his companion.

The horseman had jerked his mount to a halt and sat staring. Slade recognized Jeff Meader. He stepped into view and shouted.

"Come ahead, everything is under control." He turned anxiously toward the sheriff who was wringing blood from his fingers.

"Just nicked my wrist," he said before Slade could speak. "Nothing to it."

A quick examination told El Halcón that

164

the wound was really superficial.

"Take care of it when we get back down below," he said.

Meader came charging up to draw rein beside them.

"What in blazes!" he exclaimed. "What was all the shooting I heard."

"You were darn lucky to be in shape to hear it," said the sheriff. "See those two rifles on the ground beside those dead varmints? They were both lined with you and if Walt hadn't acted like a lightning flash in a hurry, you would have collected a slug from each of 'em."

Meader's eyes widened and he wet his suddenly dry lips with his tongue.

"Mr. Slade," he said in a strained voice, "it looks like saving my life is getting to be a habit with you."

"Always glad to oblige," Slade replied cheerfully, welcoming a chance to relieve the tension. "And in a way I felt responsible, seeing as it was a case of mistaken identity."

"Yes. The devils were laying for me, not you."

"And you are close to Walt's height and were riding a dark-colored horse," the sheriff put in. "So they figured you for him. Understand?"

"Yes, I guess I do," Meader said. "But just

the same I'm mighty, mighty beholden."

Briefly, Slade explained how he and the sheriff happened to be on hand at such an opportune moment.

"And now let's locate the horses that pair rode and load 'em up," he concluded.

The horses were quickly found, tethered to nearby branches. And after giving the bodies a brief once-over, they secured them to the saddles.

"Mean-looking cusses," said Carter, wiping his fingers on a dead outlaw's shirt.

"About average, like the others, only rather more intelligent appearing, like the others," Slade said. "We'll examine them more closely later. Now let's get down below to our own cayuses. How'd you happen to be riding over this way, Mr. Meader?"

"Taking a short cut to my spread," the rancher explained. "One of the old hands who stayed with me when I bought the holding showed me this way in and out of the Valley; I've often ridden it. Besides, Deputy Grumley told me you fellers were riding over this way, and I thought maybe I could meet up with you."

"Well, you did," the sheriff offered dryly.

"Yep, I sure did," replied Meader, drawing a deep breath. "And I'm mighty, mighty glad I did."

Reaching the Valley floor, Slade and the sheriff mounted and resumed their interrupted trip to the west. Meader elected to accompany them for a few miles and leave the Valley by way of another ascent with which he was familiar, after again thanking Slade profusely for keeping him from meeting an untimely end.

Slade and the sheriff paused at Estaban's cabin to acquaint him with their adventure.

"Ever El Halcón's way," said the Mexican. "Ever others he helps. When you return, there will be food on the table, and coffee steaming hot."

"And that's ever Estaban's way, a paragon of hospitality," Slade smiled.

SIXTEEN

Without mishap, they reached the Quijano's place and after loading up the body of the outlaw who got his comeuppance the night before and chatting for a brief period, they returned to Estaban's cabin and a bounteous repast.

"Never saw those three before," remarked Carter, whose slight wrist wound Slade had treated and bandaged. "None of the four you saw working on the rig eh?"

"That's right," Slade agreed.

"The hellion must be gettin' mighty short of hired hands that's sure for certain," Carter remarked.

"But because we have not yet corralled any of the derrick workers, we know that he has at least four," Slade pointed out. "And four with him makes a host. We've still got our work cut out for us."

"Just a matter of time," the sheriff predicted. "Just a matter of time."

With the sun low in the western sky, they said goodbye to Estaban and headed for Amarillo, making slow going of it with the four led horses, but both feeling it hadn't been such a bad day after all.

"Sorta funny, wasn't it, that Meader should happen along right when he did," Carter suddenly remarked.

"On the face, it appeared to be a remarkable coincidence," Slade replied. "However, it was really just a case of the working of the law of averages. Meader admitted that he often rode this way when heading home. And Grumley informing him we were over here somewhere decided him to follow this particular route today."

"Guess you're right," agreed the sheriff, "but it almost seems that something bigger than any of us had a hand in it."

"And that could be, too," Slade conceded soberly.

It was past midnight when they finally reached the Cowboy Capital. But late though it was, there were plenty of people on the streets and they collected quite a following on the way to the sheriff's office. That provided the volunteers to help unload the bodies and place them on the floor.

There followed a barrage of questions. Carter, a good narrator when he took the notion, obliged with a vivid, and, Slade thought, highly colored account of the episodes by way of which the bodies were acquired. Slade was showered with praise he felt he could dispense with.

"The vingaroon picked a good nickname for himself," one oldtimer remarked sententiously. "Muerto — dead man! Yep, that's just what he'll end up being. Keep up the good work, Mr. Slade, keep up the good work."

This time several of those who inspected the bodies were confident they had seen one or the other of the drygulchers hanging around town. To which, however, Slade attached little importance. He knew his man, which was all that really counted.

Finally the sheriff shooed out the stragglers and closed the door. He and Slade went through the dead men's pockets and uncovered a sizeable amount of money but nothing else the Ranger considered of significance.

"Yes, they've all been cowhands, at one time or another," Slade replied to a question from Carter. "Not recently, however."

"Anyhow, the county treasury's getting rich," Carter said, stowing the *dinero* in his safe. He chuckled.

"Imagine Meader is still getting the shakes when he thinks of those two long guns lined with him," he observed.

"In a way, he did us a favor," Slade commented. "The devils were concentrating on him, thinking he was their intended target, and were thrown completely off balance when they heard us behind them. The one whose slug nicked your hand didn't even take aim, just pitched his rifle forward and squeezed trigger."

"Which may have been lucky for one of us," the sheriff observed. "Well, suppose we amble over to the Trail End for a snack. I feel the need of a snort or two. Been quite a busy day. Hello! Here comes Grumley; he can look after those three critters and find a place to stable 'em."

Which the deputy promised to do.

After caring for their own mounts, Slade

and the sheriff made their way to the Trail End and a session with Swivel-eye Sanders, for whose benefit the sheriff repeated his account of the day's stirring happenings.

While Carter talked, Slade was thinking things over. He was beginning to feel that never had he had such an opponent as Watson Gaynard, not even excepting the infamous Veck Sosna, leader of the Comancheros, whom he had chased all over Texas and part of Mexico before dropping a loop on him via a bullet from one of his Colts.

He was of the opinion that Gaynard had more brains than Sosna, his thought processes faster, and he certainly was just as vindictive and callous where human life was concerned.

Keeping a jump ahead of the cagey rapscallion was something of a chore, but so far he had been able to do so.

He was brought back to his immediate surroundings by the arrival of their snack and put Muerto Gaynard out of his mind, for the time being.

However, the horned toad insisted on creeping back, which Slade found distinctly irritating.

"Well, how goes it?" asked the sheriff, pushing aside his empty plate and hammering for a snort.

"It doesn't," Slade replied morosely. "It seems all I do is dodge traps the sidewinder sets for me. I never encountered such a persistent devil."

"Which means he takes you plumb serious," Carter remarked.

"Yes," Slade agreed. "Of course what he fears is that some way I'll put a halt on his big objective, which to him is of much greater importance than his robbing and widelooping."

"And that is?" prompted the sheriff.

"If he manages to sink his well and bring in a really good flow of water, which he will, all right; the businessmen he has interested, not knowing the water is drawn from the Amarillo Lake underflow, will conclude he knows what he is talking about and will be all set to back him to the limit in the project of sinking a number of wells, which he has no intention of doing. Pleading necessary expenses, which will appear logical, he'll collect a nice fat advance payment from them, far more than what all his depredations have accrued. Then he'll pull out, leaving them holding the bag, an empty bag.

"See what I mean? Now what am I going to do, expose him and save the businessmen their money? Sounds good. But if I do, he'll go scotfree so far as his killings and

172

robbings are concerned, and start operating someplace else. And after all, I'm a Texas Ranger, sent here for the express purpose of curbing his criminal acts and bringing him to justice. Beginning to understand?"

"Puts you on something of a spot," conceded the sheriff.

"Yes, it does," Slade agreed. "And it is highly doubtful that he could be convicted even of fraud. For, as I mentioned before, he could insist that he just made an honest mistake. He could plead ignorance — not knowing about the underflow from the lake, and he would in all likelihood make it stick; you can't jail a man for making an honest mistake.

"And in fact, I have not the slightest desire to convict of mere fraud a man guilty of mass murder. So what we've got to somehow do is corral him before he gets the chance to bilk the businessmen out of their money."

"Yep, that's all," growled the sheriff, adding cheerfully, "my money's still on El Halcón. Do you figure Gaynard's got some more hellions on top besides the four working on the rig?"

"Yes, I do," Slade replied. "He wouldn't use those four on a raid except as a last resort; too many people in town know them and would recognize them. Remember, two of the three who set fire to Quijano's cabin escaped. And so did all three who attacked Jeff Meader outside Thankful Yates' place. The two who tried to drygulch us may be of their number, although I hardly think so. And be that as it may, there would be three, aside from the four rig workers, we know of able to navigate."

"Which is too darn many," growled the sheriff. "But maybe he will take a notion to run some cows and give us a chance to twirl a loop."

"Yes, that would help," Slade agreed. "Especially if luck will give us a break and he handles the chore in person."

"But then again, with the boys patrolling their spreads as they are, he might decide to lay off cows for a while," added Carter.

"That also is possible," Slade conceded.

Which would prove to be an under-estimate of the resourceful shrewdness of Watson Gaynard.

Deputy Grumley strolled in, having cared for the outlaws' horses, and accepted a drink.

"Forgot to mention it, with all the excitement, but Gaynard and his bunch weren't working on the rig late today," he said. "They all knocked off early."

"And that could mean something, don't you think, Walt?" Carter observed.

"Yes, it could," Slade admitted. "Of course they could have run out of material or something and are awaiting a delayed shipment, or just decided to take the evening off, but it's something to keep in mind, against the chance of something happening."

"That's the way I felt about it and figured you'd oughta know," interjected Grumley. "Hope so. You two fellers are having all the fun; me and Tom Balch don't get in on anything."

"You may get in deeper than you'll like, sooner or later," the sheriff remarked grimly. "I got a feeling in my bones that something is going to cut loose, and soon. Getting as bad as Walt when it comes to hunches, only mine are usually loco."

Grumley laughed, downed his snort and departed to look things over before going to bed. A little later, Slade and the sheriff also decided to call it a night, unaware of the stirring events taking place elsewhere.

SEVENTEEN

The ranch owners were indeed vigilantly patrolling their holdings. They were thoroughly fed up with losses and were determined to prevent, if possible, further raids on their property. Every night alert hands rode the range on the lookout for anything suspicious.

On John Fletcher's south pasture, well to the west, the two rannies on patrol gazed complacently at the cattle grazing or lying down around two big waterholes.

"Everything 'pears okay here," one remarked. "I don't figure there's much chance of anything happening this far south. Up nearer Meader's land is where something is liable to cut loose."

"I feel the same way about it," replied his partner.

"So suppose we amble up that way a piece for a look-see," suggested the first speaker.

"A notion," the other agreed. "Let's go."

The two punchers rode slowly, shooting glances in every direction, alert for anything that didn't look just right, but chatting blithely the while, their talk chiefly dealing with such mundane matters as drinks, cards, and dance floor girls, particularly the latter.

The night was pleasantly cool, with a sky of brilliant stars, and they enjoyed their patrol stint, which would relieve them of the heat and dust of the morrow. They would be snoozing comfortably while their fellows were busy at various chores.

A couple of miles passed, with the prairie lonely and deserted, so far as human occupancy was concerned.

"A bit farther and maybe we'd better turn back," one remarked.

"Guess so," the other agreed, his gaze fixed on a straggle of chaparral a few hundred yards to the right, which they were passing. There were quite a few such stands on Fletcher's northwest pastures.

"Hey!" he suddenly exclaimed. "Cal, there's somebody, a couple of somebodies riding along the edge of the brush. See 'em?"

"Yes, I do," Cal replied. "Wonder who they could be? Not some of our boys, that's sure."

"I dunno," said his companion, "but they sure ain't got any business riding out here at this time of night." He loosened the Winchester in his saddle boot as he spoke. Cal did likewise.

"Think they've spotted us, Buck?" he asked.

"Don't seem to look back any, just riding along north," answered Buck.

"Think maybe we'd better keep an eye on them for a spell?"

"Yes, I do. No telling what they may be up to. Come to think of it, they're riding right in line with a couple of big waterholes up toward Meader's holding, where there's always a bunch of cows hangin' around. Could be figurin' on grabbin' off a few head and runnin' west across Meader's land. I've always believed that's the way the cows we've lost go, no matter what Fletcher says. Yep, we'll just mosey along as if we don't know from nothing, and keep our eyes open. Keep your long gun ready to pull, too. You never can tell in this blasted section, 'specially at night."

"I've got it in front of me, ready for business," Cal said. "Watch close and see if they turn around."

However, the two mysterious horsemen did not turn but kept right on riding at a steady gait, the two cowboys keeping pace, alert and watchful.

The miles flowed back, quite a few of them, and the end of the chaparral belt came into view. Also, the two waterholes, reflecting the starlight, were dimly visible, with cattle clumped around them.

"They're after the cows!" Cal exclaimed exultantly. "We'll get 'em!"

Abruptly, the two night riders speeded up. In a couple of moments they were racing

178

their mounts. They passed the waterholes and kept right on going without slackening speed.

"What in the blinkin' blue blazes!" exclaimed Cal.

Buck, the quicker witted of the two, jerked his horse to a halt and swore bitterly.

"I'll tell you what," he replied. "Those two hellions fooled us into followin' them, to get us away from the cows around those holes to the south. Wanta bet there'll be any beefs around those holes when we get back down there? I'll take the bet for as much as you want to put out."

Cal added his own quota of profanity as they turned their cayuses and sent them speeding south.

When they finally reached the waterholes in question, Buck's prediction was verified; there was not a cow in sight.

"And there was nigh onto a hundred head!" growled Cal. "Now what?"

"To the casa and try to explain how we were made damn fools of," replied Buck.

"Think we might rouse the boys and catch the devils up?" Cal asked as they got their lathered horses under way.

"With the head start the blankety-blank-blanks have got?" Buck replied derisively. "Them cows are in the blasted Valley and way toward the New Mexico hills by now, or holed up someplace nobody knows about."

Dawn was streaking the sky with rose and gold when the shamefaced patrol reached the ranchhouse and told the story of how they had been made terrapin-brains of.

Old John Fletcher, the owner, refrained from scolding them.

"Anybody can have something put over on 'em," he said. "Head one of the boys to town to tell Brian Carter about it. Him and Slade wanted to be notified right off if something like this happened.

"And I ain't sure those cows are gone for good," he added. "I've a notion Slade has something in mind he ain't mentioned to anybody, and if he has, gentlemen, hush!

"Tell the boy to grab off a bite to eat before he rides — the cook's already stirring his stumps — and not to hurry back. Might as well spend a little time in town while he's at it."

Which was an example of the reasons John Fletcher's hands always gave their best, and were ready to fight for him, if necessary.

It was quite a ride from Fletcher's place to Amarillo and it was nearly midmorning when the cowboy arrived in town to find Sheriff Carter, an early riser, already in his office. He listened to what the hand had to tell, commented briefly.

"We'll see what we can do," he concluded.

Being thoroughly familiar with Slade's plan, he knew there was no hurry and dawdled over his breakfast before rousing the Ranger.

"Looks like this might be it," he commented.

"Yes, it does," El Halcón agreed. "We won't start out until the afternoon is along! Guess you and I and the deputies should be all that's needed."

"Especially with the element of surprise working on our side," said Carter.

While Slade was eating, Deputy Grumley dropped in.

"Still no work on that drilling rig," he announced. "Didn't see anything of Gaynard, either."

"Which is good hearing," Slade said. "Looks like the sidewinder is handling the chore in person. Was a clever trick he pulled last night, luring the patrol to the north while the rest of the bunch rounded up the cows around the south waterholes and shoved them in a straight line to the Valley and that cave, where they're holed up right now, or all signs fail."

"Still figure he hasn't tumbled to the fact

that you've located his hole-in-the-wall?" asked Carter.

"I don't think he has," Slade replied. "If I'm wrong, we may find ourselves hanging onto the hot end of the branding iron and wishing we could let go," he added grimly.

His hearers looked a mite uncomfortable. Which, under the circumstances, was not strange.

"Oh, I reckon we'll make out," Carter said at length. "If you figure he hasn't caught on, he hasn't."

"Hope you're right," Slade replied. "We'll find out before the night is over."

The day wore on, another nice day with an autumn crispness to the air. The faraway hills were rose-lighted on the billowy slopes, and pearl in the deep clefts. The lordly form of Tucumcari was shrouded in indigo against a flame of orange. The rangeland was an endless ocean of amethyst. A day that made one glad to be alive.

Carter, the deputies and Slade sat in the office and smoked and talked, the latter with an eye to the clock. Noon came and went and he stood up, stretching his long arms above his head.

"Guess we'd better get moving," he said. "Best not to push our cayuses too hard; may

182

need all they have to give later on. Always the chance that the hellions, feeling safe from observation, may leave their hole-up a bit early and we'll be forced to run them down before they reach the hills. Of course we have no official standing in New Mexico, but I figure we can risk that. All set? Let's go!"

"I can't get over the way those squirrel-brains fell for that Muerto trick," the sheriff grumbled as they made their way to the stable, referring to the duped patrol of the night before.

"*Amigo* Gaynard is without doubt a profound student of human nature and knows with whom he deals," Slade answered. "Cowhands, as a rule, are not overly gifted with imagination and it was logical for them to conclude those two riders were up to no good and that they'd better keep an eye on them. Concentrating on the riders they gave no thought to how far they were being lured north and forgot all about the cows at the south waterholes. So don't be too hard on them."

"Guess I shouldn't be," Carter agreed. "Chances are I'd have been bamboozled the same way."

Cinching up, they rode due north toward the Canadian River Valley, but a few miles from the depression, Slade turned sharply west.

"I think we're safe in pursuing this route," he explained. "The outer mouth of the cave is well to the south of the Valley wall, so we can't reach it by following the trend of the Valley. I'd say the hellions are unlikely to have somebody outside keeping watch, feeling secure in their hidden hole-up. That brush covered ridge stretches quite a ways to the east and when we reach it, we'll crowd in close to the growth, where there is little chance of us being observed unless somebody rides well out on the prairie."

"Sounds reasonable," he said. "Anyhow, you're running the shebang and what you say goes."

They rode steadily at a fair pace, Slade constantly scanning the prairie in every direction, casting an occasional glance at the sun dipping down the western sky.

Finally, with the New Mexico hills looming large, the brush-grown ridge in question came into view. A little later they reached it, sidling their horses against the growth, which was already becoming shadowy. Slade slowed the pace, and then still more, studying the terrain ahead.

Quite a bit farther on, he called a halt, and for some moments sat gazing along the line of the growth.

"Here we leave the horses," he said. "Into the brush with them. Conditions being what they are, I figure we'll be better on our feet. They are still in the cave, all right; the cut brush that screens the opening hasn't been removed. They'll remove it first, of course, and I'll spot them doing it. Then they'll mount and drive the herd through, all set to keep it from scattering. They'll be bunched behind the cows and the moment they show will be the time to hit them. That way the herd will block any attempt at escaping to the hills.

"You do the talking, Brian, we must give them their chance to surrender. They won't give up without a fight, so don't waste a shot. It's a killer bunch and we can expect no mercy if they get the upper hand. All right, here we go."

At a snail-crawl they moved ahead, careful not to make the slightest sound. A hundred yards and a little better and Slade held up his hand. The posse halted to stand motionless, waiting.

The sun had set and the shadows were deepening. As the minutes passed, Slade began growing uneasy; full dark would be to their disadvantage.

And then, only a few yards ahead, Slade's

eyes detected the top of a bush begin moving, vanish from sight. Another, and still another; then all motion ceased.

"Get ready!" he breathed. The posse clutched their weapons.

Again motion, and through the opening streamed the shadowy shapes of the cattle, fanning out when they reached the open prairie. Another moment and four horsemen loomed behind the last stragglers. Slade nudged the sheriff. The old peace officer's voice blared above the beat of the hoofs.

"Elevate! In the name of the law!"

Startled exclamations. The blur of turning faces. The gleam of shifted metal!

"Let them have it!" Slade roared. And the ball was open!

Smoke and flame! The booming of the guns! Shouts, curses! The bawling of the frightened cattle! Slade, shooting with both hands, saw a man spin from his saddle. And he saw a second outlaw whirl his horse and go streaking back through the opening.

Heedless of the blazing outlaw guns, Slade bounded forward, slugs fanning his face. He whisked through the opening and raced toward the cave mouth, guns ready to sweep the narrow bore from side to side with lead.

Then he rocked on his heels, sprang

backward in a catlike leap as, right in front of him, the massive overhang fell with a thunderous crash, completely blocking the mouth of the cave.

EIGHTEEN

Peppered by bits of flying stone, a cloud of dust swirling about him, Slade realized that outside the shooting had stopped. Sheriff Carter burst into view, waving his gun.

"Got all three of them!" he whooped. "You all right? How'd you make out?"

"The Devil himself must look after that sidewinder!" Slade replied wrathfully, glowering at the mass of splintered rock. "Couldn't think of anything else, so he pulls a mountain down in front of me!"

"It was Muerto?"

"Of course," Slade said. "That hairtrigger brain of his! Always does the right thing at just the right moment. I thought I had him in that narrow passage, and then down came that blasted overhang, loosened by the vibrations set up by the shooting, and blocked me. Oh, well, maybe his luck will run out some day."

The sheriff repeated one of his favorite remarks where El Halcón was concerned, "Just a matter of time, just a matter of time."

"Anybody hurt?" Slade asked.

"Oh, Balch has a little skin knocked off his ribs, nothing to bother about, hardly bleeding. They spoiled my left shirt sleeve and blew a hole through the top of Grumley's hat. That's all. As you figured, they were caught plumb off balance and shot wild."

"All except Gaynard," Slade grumbled. "He's never off balance."

"Come out and see what we bagged," Carter suggested. "I think you did for the first one."

Somebody had fetched a sotol stalk and by its light, Slade examined Balch's bullet-creased ribs and concluded the wound was of little consequence.

"Take care of it shortly," he said, and whistled a loud, clear note.

While waiting for Shadow to arrive, which he did a few moments later, snorting inquiringly, Slade inspected the dead outlaws and shook his head.

"No member of the rigging crew present," he said. "Wouldn't be surprised if the pair that duped Fletcher's patrolling cowhands last night were two of them. Perhaps the other two helped round up the cows and shove them into the cave, and then headed for town where, the chances are, we'll find them at work on the rig tomorrow.

"And with Gaynard bossing the job," he added disgustedly.

"Looks like the horned toad may have more men at his back than we figured," the sheriff remarked.

"Yes, the Devil alone knows how many," Slade replied. "Of course, if he felt the need of replacements he could find plenty in this section."

"It's crawlin' with 'em," growled Carter.

Balch's slight injury was cared for. The outlaw horses, which had run but a short distance, were caught, the bodies loaded onto them. Slade gazed at the cattle; they had quieted and were grazing.

"Grumley can cut across the Valley, farther east and tell Fletcher where to find them," he decided. "And you might as well spend the rest of the night at his casa, Grumley. Well, guess we are all set to head for town."

"Doc Beard will have quite a collection to set on," chuckled Carter. "I told him to put off the inquest on those other horned toads."

Daybreak was near when they reached Amarillo. The bodies were placed on the office floor besides the others, the worn-out horses cared for, and everybody tumbled into bed.

It was past noon when Slade awoke, feeling greatly refreshed and much better in various ways. He yawned, stretched and before getting up, reviewed in his mind the recent happenings. He had recovered from his irritation over Gaynard's almost miraculous escape and concluded it hadn't been such a bad night, after all. Three more devils taken care of. And there wouldn't be any more widelooped cows run through that hole in the wall; it was securely blocked by the fall of the overhang. Nothing short of dynamite in large quantities would open it. And he didn't give even Gaynard credit for attempting such a caper.

He bathed, shaved, donned a clean shirt and overalls and headed for the Trail End and breakfast, where he found rugged old Sheriff Carter awaiting him.

"When you get old you don't need much sleep, as you'll find out some day. That is, if you manage to stay in one piece that long," was the sheriff's reply to Slade's comment on his early rising. "Now you're here at last, let's eat."

Which they proceeded to do, in leisurely comfort, Swivel-eye not allowing them to be pestered by questions.

It was different at the office, however, where Deputy Balch was holding sway and regaling eager listeners with a colorful account of the night's incidents, giving Slade all the credit due him.

Rather more than what was due, El Halcón felt, answering the barrage of questions hurled at him briefly and to the point.

Several individuals maintained they had seen all three of the outlaws in town at one time or another but were vague as to just where and under what circumstances. Which was what Slade expected.

Finally, knowing the inquest would not be held until late, he managed to escape from his admirers and walked to where he had a view of the lake.

As he also expected, the drill riggers were on the job, with Watson Gaynard superintending matters. Another day, he estimated, and the derrick would be completed, the cable reeved over the pulley at the top, and the drilling ready to begin. Looked like he was going to have to work fast were the businessmen's money to be saved and a loop dropped on his slippery quarry.

For his opinion that Gaynard really did intend to pull out of the section after making his big haul was crystallizing. Yes, he must work fast, and at the moment he had not the slightest idea which way to turn. Looked like that again he could only wait, and let events shape their course, hoping they would present opportunity.

He did not approach the drilling site but continued to the Washout for a word with Thankful Yates, who might have something to tell him, although he was not too sanguine as to that.

Over a drink, Slade detailed briefly the happenings of the night before. To which the saloon keeper listened with absorbed interest.

"Well, one thing is sure for certain," he said when the Ranger paused, "folks are now lookin' on Muerto as a joke. Even the Mexican boys, who were dubious about the rapscallion till you showed up. Now everybody is laughing at the notion he's an evil spirit crawled out of the grave to work his hellishness."

"Just the same, he's still a long ways from being a joke," Slade differed. "He's vicious, ruthless, and capable. I fear we'll be hearing from him again soon.

"That is one of the reasons why such characters flourish. Let them suffer a few setbacks and people are prone to write them off as of no further consequence. Whereas the exact opposite is true. They merely become more vindictive and resourceful. Until Muerto himself is corralled, we can look for more trouble."

To which Thankful nodded sober agreement, but said, "Well, anyhow, with El Halcón on the job, I'm mighty of the opinion that Muerto is close to the end of his twine."

Doc Beard held his inquest. The jury's verdict was that the killing of the outlaws was justified.

After the inquest, restless and uneasy, Slade left the office again. He experienced a growing premonition that something untoward was due to happen.

Now, although it was not very late, there was no activity at the drill rig; evidently the workers had knocked off early. Which didn't help.

He drew some comfort from watching the glory of the sunset and the lovely transition of day to night. But that was only temporary; the impact of the unpleasant presentiment returned in full force.

Oh, well, perhaps something to eat and a drink would tend to lessen the tension of his strung nerves. He turned his steps to the Trail End.

There he found Brian Carter already at a table, discussing a snort of redeye.

"Figured you'd be along soon," the sheriff said. "Take a load off your feet and feed your tapeworm. Looks like a busy night. But then all of 'em are in this blasted rum-hole. What a bunch of characters at the bar! Where in blazes do they all come from?"

Slade didn't know and refrained from hazarding a guess. He changed his mind about a drink and compromised for coffee, which he usually found more soothing. Carter shook his head in disapproval and ordered another snort.

Shortly their dinner arrived and despite his disturbed state of mind, Slade set to it with apetite. One advantage of being young and brimming with lusty life; food always had an attraction and helped to relegate moodiness to the background, for the time being, at least.

All of which meant that El Halcón was searching the cracks and crannies of his mind for a hunch. Which so far had eluded him.

"A darn shame we didn't get a good look at that blasted Gaynard last night," the sheriff suddenly remarked. "That would have tied him up with the bunch."

"Yes, it would have helped," Slade agreed. "But there was no distinguishing features in that light, or lack of it. All I could say is that he looked to be Gaynard's build, and you can't take that into court."

"Sidewinders sure seem to get the breaks," Carter growled. "Oh, well, another time."

Swivel-eye came over and joined them for a few minutes.

"Don't see many familiar faces tonight," Slade observed, glancing around.

"Mostly new fellers, quite a few I don't remember seeing before," Swivel replied. "Mr. Gaynard was in a little while ago. Said he knocked off work early. That his derrick is finished and all set to start drilling if it wasn't that some drilling tools that should have been here already hadn't showed up yet. Said he wired the dealers and they promised to have them here in a day or two. Said he aimed to ride around a bit and spot some more places to sink holes. Sure knows his business, all right."

"Yes, he does," Slade agreed dryly, with a significance that was lost on Swivel-eye.

"The hellion is up to something, sure as blazes," Carter declared, after the owner had moved back to the bar.

"Yes, I think you're right," Slade replied. "I looked things over pretty closely when I was there, and I'm willing to wager he doesn't lack drilling tools. Gives him a nice excuse for being off the job for a while. Yes, Swivel-eye is right, he knows his business. And we are likely to hear about that 'business' before long."

"What *could* the hellion have in mind?" Carter wondered.

"You should be more familiar with the section than I am, so suppose you do some guessing," Slade suggested.

"My mind's empty as a drum!" the sheriff lamented. "There are so many things he could hit — stages, banks, cow trains, saloons, stores. It's like trying to pick a particular tick off a sheep's back, with the sheep not agreein' to stand still."

Slade laughed, although he was not in much of a mood for mirth, and ordered more coffee.

The night wore on, with nothing untoward happening, so far as El Halcón and the sheriff knew. But because one's own door is shut doesn't mean the whole world's warm.

"Hello!" Carter exclaimed. "Here comes Jeff Meader."

He beckoned the Triangle M owner to join them.

Meader did so, accepted a chair and a drink. "Been down at the Washout all evening," he announced. "I like that place. Always interesting and lively."

196

"Too darn lively at times," grunted the sheriff.

"By the way," Meader remarked after a few minutes of desultory conversation, "I saw Watson Gaynard and four fellers riding north across the Valley just before dark. Wonder where they were headed?"

"Did they see you?" Slade asked quickly.

"Don't think so," Meader replied. "They were quite a ways off, talking together, and didn't look my way. I just got a glimpse of them through the brush, but I recognized Gaynard. No, I don't think they saw me."

Slade deftly changed the subject before the rancher could wonder why he asked. He thought it was probably lucky for Meader that they didn't see him.

Meader ordered a round, downed his, and said, "I'm calling it a night; got a business appointment for noon. That's why I came in tonight. Be seeing you both."

As they watched him pass through the swinging doors, the sheriff demanded querulously, "Now, where in blazes were those wind spiders headed?"

"I'd like to have the answer," Slade said. "I predict we'll learn soon enough. They were up to no good, that's sure for certain. I'm not positive, but I'd not be one bit surprised if they were on their way to Dumas. If Meader had contacted us earlier in the evening, we might have made a try for them. Too late now, however. Very likely anything they might have had in mind is already consummated and they're in the clear."

"By gosh! I believe you may have hit it," exclaimed the sheriff. "Well, once again not in my bailiwick; they can't blame us."

"No, but I blame myself for letting that cunning devil put another one over," Slade returned morosely.

"For the love of Pete! Nobody can think of everything ahead of time," snorted Carter. "Not even El Halcón."

"That's comforting," Slade smiled. "Keep on talking."

The sheriff gave a disgusted grunt and failed to oblige.

"Yes, I've a hunch that whatever they have in mind they are putting into operation just about now," Slade said. "And if they are, I'll wager they are masked with not a chance that anybody would be able to identify them. That is if anybody happens to get a glimpse of them, which is improbable.

"And," he added, "if they desire to, they can ride right into town, open and above-board, and there won't be a thing we can do about it."

"Maybe they'll slip up somehow and get their comeuppance," Carter said hopefully.

"Possible, but highly improbable," Slade replied. "Our *amigo* Muerto isn't much given to making slips."

"He's made a few, or some of his bunch have," the sheriff pointed out. "That is, with a little help from El Halcón."

"Oh, he is not infallible, of course," Slade conceded. "Nobody is, but he comes unpleasantly close to it. Well, I guess we might as well stop beating our empty skulls, emulate Jeff Meader's example, and go to bed."

"A notion," agreed Carter.

They proceeded to put it into effect, in no very equable frame of mind.

NINETEEN

Southeast of Dalhart, the trail to Amarillo ran through a windswept region of seemingly endless prairies. There was not a tree to be seen, only the far-flung vista of rippling grass heads that were like to advancing and retreating shadows in the vagaries of the breeze.

All the long afternoon, the stage from Dalhart rolled steadily through the golden sunglow. Beside the driver sat an armed guard who certainly didn't expect to do any business between Dalhart and Dumas. Not on that vast open plain where an advancing horseman could be seen for miles. He and the driver joked and chatted, the reins slack on the backs of the four sturdy horses that drew the vehicle and looked forward to oats in the near future.

Just as dusk was falling, the big coach reached Dumas and paused before the stage station. The horses were cared for, the guard and the driver entered a nearby restaurant and saloon in search of refreshment and something to eat, with the prospect of a pleasant evening and a good night's rest in the offing. Not until after daybreak would the stage continue on the last lap of the trip to Amarillo.

South of Dumas, the terrain was different, the trail winding into a stretch of country broken by ravines and gulches some dry, others with little creeks twisting toward the Canadian River. Where the guard and his partner locked inside the coach would be watchful and vigilant. For from Dumas the stage would be packing quite a large sum of money consigned to the Amarillo bank.

Dumas was a bustling cowtown. Later, agriculture would add to its prosperity, and still later it would thrive on oil developments. At present, however, cattle were dominant.

The stage station set a little apart from other buildings. On one side was a growth of tall trees, under which the shadows were already deep.

The hours jogged along. Midnight came and went. An hour passed, and another. Now the streets were deserted. Only in the saloons, one of which was not far from the station, was there activity.

In the station office, the night watchman, an elderly but capable individual, was having his snack. He sat with his back to the door. The lamp was turned low and the office was cozy and comfortable. The watchman discussed his late lunch and coffee with relish.

Had he not been so occupied with his food, he might have heard the tiny click of a turned key from the direction of the door. Silently the door opened a crack. Slowly, silently, the crack widened. Through the opening glided five masked men, the last softly closed the door.

The slight sound of the closing door caused the watchman to raise his head, half turn in his chair. A gun barrel crashed against his skull and laid him senseless on the floor. Two of the masked men took up stations near the door, one on either side, a third by the window. The others stepped over the body of the watchman and approached the big old iron safe in a corner of the room. One, a tall, broad-shouldered and powerfully built person, squatted before the safe door. His companion passed him a hand drill and there followed but the smallest of sounds, as if a rat with metal teeth was gnawing under the floor boards.

A couple of moments and a hole was drilled beside the combination knob, the chilled steel bit cutting through the soft iron as if it were cheese. Another overlapping hole followed, and another, another, and still another. The combination knob was lifted out, the door swung open. A small jimmy took care of the locked inner drawers. The robber began transferring packets of bills and rolls of gold coin from the drawers to a sack his companion handed him. Everything was going like clockwork.

But what the outlaws didn't know, one of the stage guards slept in a little cubbyhole room in the back of the building.

A sound, perhaps the slight thud of the combination knob dropped to the floor, or the creak of the manipulated jimmy, awoke the guard. For a moment he lay listening. Then he slipped from his couch, seized his gun, which lay ready to hand, and glided to the office door.

His mistake was in not instantly starting shooting. Instead, with his iron up and lined, he called out, "What the devil's going on here? Get your hands up!"

The robbers whirled, and the office fairly exploded with a roar of gunfire.

The guard tried to fight back, but fell dead after pulling trigger once, riddled with bullets. The tall man calmly finished the chore of filling the money sack. Then all five dashed to the door, flung it open and darted through, heading for the shadows under the trees.

In the nearby saloon, the bellow of gunfire had been heard and men were streaming out, shouting questions.

From under the trees bulged five horsemen, swerving their mounts into the street, which ran west, scattering the yelling crowd that dived wildly to escape the clashing hoofs. A quick-witted individual jerked a gun and squeezed the trigger. But the slug missed.

The robbers, twisting in their saddles, poured back answering lead that did not find a mark. Then they whisked around a corner and were gone, the beat of hoofs dimming into the south.

Realizing what had happened, men hurried into the station and took in the situation at a glance. The doctor was sent for to care for the injured night watchman. The sheriff was summoned. When he arrived, he hastily got a posse together and rode in fruitless pursuit of the outlaws.

"Yes, they've got a big head start," he conceded, "but you never can tell, something might slow them up. I had a thing like that happen once. Bagged me a couple of hellions. Let's go!"

"I figure they'll be heading for the Canadian Valley," he added. "We'll see."

Alert and vigilant, they rode at a fast pace through the broken country. A very peaceful ride so far as contacting outlaws were concerned. With the sun peeping over the edge of the world, they drew rein at the lip of the Valley.

"Yep, they gave us the slip," the sheriff admitted. "No trailing them in that blasted gulch. Well, this is one of the easiest crossings, so I reckon we might as well keep on going to Amarillo and notify Brian Carter. We're in Potter County, now, his bailiwick. Maybe he can think of something."

Carter and Slade were in the office when the posse arrived with the story of what happened in Dumas. Carter swore in weary disgust, but El Halcón evinced not the least surprise at what the Moore County sheriff had to tell them.

"Five in the bunch, I believe you said," he remarked. "And all were masked?"

"That's right," the sheriff replied. "That's what folks who saw them skalleyhoot out of town said. The station watchman got his senses back just before we left — not too bad hurt — but couldn't say how many there were. Clobbered him before he got a real look, I reckon."

"Well, we'll do what we can," Sheriff Carter promised. "May not be too much, but you never can tell for sure. Okay, we'll show you a stable that will look after your nags, and then you might as well come along with us to the Trail End for a surrounding. Slade and I haven't had breakfast yet."

He did not explain that the reason why they didn't eat as soon as they awakened was because Slade expected word from Dumas at any moment.

At the Trail End, several of the posse paused at the bar for a drink and the story of the Dumas outrage was soon spread around, to the accompaniment of wild guesses and conjecture.

"Nope, I don't know for sure how much they tied onto, must have been quite a lot," the Moore County sheriff replied to a question from Carter as to the amount taken from the safe. "Was to swing some sort of a deal here in Amarillo, just what I don't know; didn't wait to get details.

"But it looks like to me that somebody here is able to learn things they're not supposed to know about."

Slade and Carter exchanged significant glances, but did not vocally comment.

After finishing their meal, the posse was packed off to the hotel and bed. Slade and Carter retired to the office to discuss matters.

The day passed peacefully, with no activity at the site of the drilling rig. Nothing happened during the night, and the next morning, Gaynard and his riggers were on the job, busily getting ready to drill. Another day or two and the bit would be churning into the earth, or so it appeared.

"Hellions must have holed up somewhere yesterday and sneaked into town after dark," Carter observed.

"Yes, and by way of my own stupidity in not guessing where, I'm afraid we missed an opportunity," Slade said.

"How's that?" Carter asked.

Slade countered with a question of his own. "Undoubtedly they did hole up some-

206

where yesterday, so where?"

"How the devil do I know?" grunted the sheriff.

Slade asked another question. "Where is the last place one would think of them holing up?"

"Oh, come on! Stop beating around the bush and tell me what's on your mind," Carter complained peevishly.

"As I've remarked before, Gaynard is a positive genius at doing what nobody would expect him to do," Slade explained. "The last logical place it would seem, after what happened there, would be that cave, which can still be entered from the Valley. You'll remember that where it widens, not far from the south, where the cows were held, is fitted up as a very comfortable hideout. I'll wager that after finishing their chore at Dumas they hightailed for the Valley and that cave. They wouldn't have wanted to be seen riding into town during the day, against the even faint chance it might tie them up with something; Gaynard thinks about everything. If I'd thought of it right after we heard about what happened at Dumas, we would have had a good opportunity to drop a loop on the whole bunch. "But I didn't think of it until late yesterday, which was of course too late. Understand?"

"Yep, I understand, and I've a notion you hit the nail on the head, but I don't see any reason why you should be beatin' yourself over the head because you didn't think of it sooner. As I've told you, nobody can think of everything, not even El Halcón."

"And I recall replying that your remark was comforting," Slade replied, with a smile. "But after a couple of inexcusable blunders on my part, the repetition begins to acquire something the nature of cold comfort."

"Now you're getting me all twisted," snorted the sheriff.

"In plain words, letting me down easy," Slade chuckled.

The sheriff gave vent to another snort and stuffed his old black pipe with black tobacco. Slade rolled a cigarette and for some time they smoked in silence, each busy with his thoughts.

Slade's were not satisfactory. For he was beset by an uneasy feeling that time was running out, with opportunities to corral the elusive Watson Gaynard dwindling. Gaynard had made two recent good hauls and might well be experiencing a quite complacent mood, with possibly soon concluding that it would be a sensible notion to let well enough alone and concentrate on the big

208

harvest he expected to reap from the gullible business people who would back his venture.

And as the days passed with nothing untoward happening, El Halcón's uneasiness became more and more pronounced. Gaynard's drilling operation was going full blast. Steam spouted from his engine exhaust, the walking beam jigged, the bit plunged deeper and deeper into the earth. Comparatively speaking, no great time would elapse till he would strike the lake underflow and start pumping water.

Walt Slade hoped fervently that opportunity would present before that took place, basing his hope on Gaynard's greed and the undoubted lure criminal operations had for the man. As a matter of fact, opportunity was in the making.

TWENTY

Cattle buyers are often eccentric individuals, although their eccentricities are usually leavened with sound common sense and they are students of human nature.

Old Ben Ord was an outstanding example of his class. Thoroughly versed in the peculiarities of cattlemen, he was well aware of the salutory effect cash laid out in plain view has on a prospective seller. Which enabled Ord to strike some excellent bargains in cattle.

So his commodious half-tented wagon, in addition to a bountiful supply of delectable provisions, old Ben being fond of creature comforts, always packed a large sum of money.

Which by way of old Ben's financial legerdemain would be transformed into fat beefs he would dispose of at a handsome profit.

Ord took no chances with his wheeled "bank" which could prove an attraction to gentlemen with their own unorthodox notions of financial transactions. So two alert outriders, skilled in the use of six-gun and rifle, always accompanied the equipage. Buyers had been murdered and robbed.

In Amarillo, things were in a state of suspended animation, as it were, for the morrow was payday again and Amarillo was, collectively and expectantly, holding its breath.

Slade noted that the workers at the drilling site had knocked off work early, which was to be expected. Around the following noon, when the cowhands from the spreads were already riding in, the railroaders streaming past the paycar window, he once more visited the drilling site. There was nobody around save an old Mexican seated on a bench, smoking a *cigarillo*. Slade approached and greeted him.

"The Señor Gaynard me hired to stoke the fire under the boiler, make sure it is properly banked, and keep watch over the machinery," the Mexican explained. "So that his *hombres* can the payday observe."

Slade chatted with him for a few minutes, then visited the Washout and various other places of celebration, including the Trail End. Nowhere were Gaynard or his hands in evidence. After a cup of coffee in the Trail End, which was already booming, Slade made his way to the sheriff's office, his eyes thoughtful.

"I'm convinced something is in the wind," he told the sheriff. "What I haven't the slightest notion, but I'm firmly of the opinion that something is. Those devils are nowhere in town, of that I am positive. Which very likely means they slipped out some time during the night."

"Yes, this may well be it. We'll try and take advantage of anything that develops. Keep your deputies handy."

"I done hired a couple of specials to patrol the town, and told Balch and Grumley to keep in touch, just in case," Carter replied.

Ben Ord rolled south from Dalhart, where he had replenished his money supply, with side stops at Channing and a couple of small villages, hardly more than a scattering of houses. Evening of the third day out from Dalhart found his wagon negotiating the final fringe of broken country south of Dumas and no great distance from the Valley. His plan was to descend into the Valley and pitch camp beside the river, then continue on to Amarillo.

The wagon was traversing a straight stretch of trail, onto which, a short distance ahead, a grass-grown and somewhat narrow ravine opened from the west. Suddenly one of the outriders, close to the wagon because of the narrowness of the brush encroached trail, flung up his head.

"What the blazes is that racket?" he exclaimed.

"Sounds like sheep," his companion replied. "Plenty of 'em graze in these ravines. But they're sure kicking up a row."

It was sheep all right. Another moment and a torrent of bleating woolly shapes streamed from the ravine, directly in front of the wagon.

The horses halted, snorting with fright, bucked, swerved, tried to turn and escape

212

the woolly tide. But old Ben had a firm grip on the reins and held them to the trail. The cursing outriders were endeavoring to shunt the panicked sheep away from the wagon.

After the sheep came five bawling horsemen. In the excitement, neither Ord nor the outriders noticed that hat-brims were pulled low, neckerchiefs pulled up high.

"Turn 'em!" one shouted. "Turn the stampedin' hellions! Turn 'em." The guards tried, with scant success.

From the ranks of the horsemen roared gunfire. Old Ben fell dead. The outriders tried to draw their irons, but died before they could clear leather. The outlaws swarmed over the wagon and quickly secured Ord's plumb money pouch.

One of the killers, tall, broad of shoulder, with glittering eyes, deliberately emptied his gun into the three bodies, making sure there was not a spark of life left. Then the killers mounted and headed south at a fast pace. Muerto had struck again!

A horrified Mexican youth, in whose care the sheep had been left and who dived into a bristle of growth, undetected when the outlaws entered the ravine where the sheep grazed saw it all. He waited until he was sure the devils were gone, then crept from his refuge.

Solicitous of animals, he took time to free the wagon horses and strip the rig from one of the dead guard's mounts. A shrewd judge of horse flesh, he chose the best of the two and sent it racing south, keeping a sharp lookout for the outlaws, and seeing nothing of them.

The evening was not far advanced when he reached Amarillo, learned the sheriff was at the Trail End. He slipped in unobtrusively, spotted the sheriff and Slade, and whispered to them the story of what he saw happen.

Slade at once beckoned Swivel-eye. "Look after this *muchacho*," he told the owner. "All the drinks he wants, or anything else. We are a lot beholden to him."

"Sure for certain, Mr. Slade," Swivel-eye replied. The boy bowed reverently to El Halcón and accompanied Swivel-eye to the bar.

"We'll want you to be around tomorrow," Slade told him in parting.

"That will I be, *Capitán*," the Mexican promised.

"Smart little coot," Slade observed. "Didn't rush in bawling what he saw. Well, we'll see if my hunch is a straight one. At least we have a witness to the killings, although it is doubtful if he could identify any of them. Never can tell, though, young

214

eyes are sharp."

"Figure it was Muerto, eh?" remarked the sheriff.

"Of course," Slade replied. "That sheep trick was typical of him."

The deputies were quickly located. The posse cinched up and rode north by west toward a descent into the Valley with which Slade was familiar.

Outside town, he drew from a cunningly concealed secret pocket in his broad leather belt the famous silver star set on a silver circle, the honored badge of the Texas Rangers, and pinned it on his shirt front.

"Just a chance the authority it packs would cause one of the devils to surrender," he explained. "I doubt it, though. That is, if we really do contact them."

"We'll contact 'em, all right," the sheriff predicted confidently. "And when we've done with them, we won't need any witnesses."

It was several hours past midnight when they reached the cave mouth. The cut brush was removed, the horses led through.

"We'll replace the bushes," Slade said. "Against the slim chance they are still outside. I'd say they are either holed up in the cave, or we're following a cold trail. I think I can judge how far we'll ride. Then we'll leave the horses and slide forward on foot. If it comes to a fight, and I predict it will, don't forget, it is a killer bunch. I'll give them a chance to surrender, then shoot fast and straight. We should have the element of surprise well in our favor; it will very likely throw them off balance for an instant. That is if we catch them flat-footed, as I think we will. Okay, let's go."

Slade set a slow pace through the bore, straining his ears for any sound that would herald the approach of the outlaws, did they conclude to leave their hole-up early, which he hardly thought they would. But with Muerto, anything could be expected.

Behind him, the posse was tense, trying to pierce the black dark from which any moment death might thunder. For it was nervous work, stealthing along with the beat of the horses' irons echoing back from the rock walls, unpleasantly loud.

Finally Slade estimated from the distance they had covered that they could risk the horses no longer. He drew rein, the others jostling to a halt.

"Here we go," he whispered as he dismounted. "Another ten minutes and it should be them, or us." He smothered a chuckle as he heard the others draw deep breath.

Forward they stole, step by slow step, peering and listening, careful not to kick any loose boulder. After what seemed to be an interminable trudge, ahead appeared a faint glow of light. Another moment and a mutter of voices was audible. El Halcón's hunch was a straight one; the outlaws were right where he had expected them to be. A smell of cooking permeated the air.

A few more cautious strides and the point where the cavern widened came into view. A big fire had been kindled and the outlaws lounged about, smoking and talking, their horses tethered at one side.

Slade stepped forward, into the circle of firelight. His voice rolled forth:

"Trail's end, Gaynard! You are under arrest! In the name of the State of Texas!"

With a yell of maniacal fury, Gaynard went for his guns. But Slade drew and shot, left and right, left and right, before he could squeeze trigger. He reeled back and back, slumped to the rock floor, his chest riddled by the Ranger's slugs.

Carter and the deputies were shooting cooly and carefully. The outlaws fired wildly in return, but caught utterly off balance by the unexpected attack, they fell, one by one.

Lowering his smoking Colts, Slade peered through the powder fog. He walked slowly forward and gazed down at the strangely composed face of the dead outlaw leader.

Watson Gaynard, the dread Muerto, had paid the ultimate penalty for his crimes.

"Well, guess that takes care of that," El Halcón said in a tired voice. "Including the four drill rig workers."

"With the finish just what I predicted all along it would be," replied Carter. "Now what?"

"Now we'll give the horses a couple of hours' rest and then head back to town with our trophies," Slade said.

"And there's lots of good chuck scattered around, and a pot of coffee," observed the cheerful Grumley. "So how about a snack while we're waiting?" He got busy over the fire.

Balch was dispatched to fetch the horses, which were supplied with a plentiful surrounding of oats from one of the sacks along the wall, the outlaw horses getting a second helping. Soon the posse, with the bodies shoved to one side, sat down to a tasty snack and plenty of coffee before tackling the long ride back to Amarillo.

Slade unpinned the Ranger badge and returned it to its pocket. "Looks like I'm still undercover," he chuckled.

It was long past daybreak when they

reached Amarillo, but there were still quite a few payday celebrants roaming the streets and a crowd followed them to the office to help lay out the bodies and be regaled with an account of the death of Watson Gaynard and his unmasking as Muerto. They hurried out to spread the news to a startled town.

After caring for the horses, Slade and the sheriff repaired to the Trail End, Carter feeling the need of a snort before going to bed. There they found a tired and anxious Jerry Norman awaiting them.

"We rode in last night right after you left," she explained. "Thank Heaven you're back safe. And by the look of you, you belong in bed," she said to Slade.

"Good hunting!" said the sheriff.

Jerry wrinkled her nose at him. "And I'm taking him to the casa tomorrow for a few days' rest," she added.

"Rest?" said the sheriff.

"Come on, Walt, and let's get out of here," she concluded. Carter shook with laughter as he watched them depart together.

That evening, several Amarillo business people conferred with Slade and the sheriff, the situation outlined for them.

"You saved us a very nice sum of money, Mr. Slade," said their spokesman. "We would like to show our appreciation in a substantial manner. You certainly deserve a reward for —"

"To be of service is reward enough," Slade smilingly interrupted. A glance at his face and the businessman held out his hand.

"By the way," remarked Carter, "my specials are fetching in the carcasses of that poor old buyer and his hands. We recovered his money, too, and I reckon we'll learn who will inherit it."

"And you gentlemen," Slade said to the business people, "will inherit a drilling rig for which I venture to predict you'll soon find use."

"Expect you have the right of it," the spokesman admitted. "We're going to need more water soon, that's sure for certain."

After again thanking Slade and shaking hands all around, they departed.

"And I suppose after a few days of — *rest,* you'll be heading back to the Post," remarked Carter.

"Yes, to learn what next Captain Jim has lined up for me," Slade replied. "But I predict I'll be back to this trouble spot before long."

"Wouldn't be surprised," conceded the sheriff.

"Jerry and I will ride to the XT spread by way of the Valley," Slade added. "So I can say goodbye to old Estaban and the Quijanos. Glad you took care of the Mexican boy who brought us word of Ord's murder."

"He can stay drunk a week," chuckled Carter. "Okay, be seeing you."

Three days later, Jerry Norman said, "Good hunting, dear. *Hasta luego* — till we meet again!"

She watched him ride away, tall and graceful atop his great black horse, to where duty called and new adventure waited.

ABOUT THE AUTHOR

Bradford Scott was a pseudonym for **Leslie Scott** who was born in Lewisburg, West Virginia. During the Great War, he joined the French Foreign Legion and spent four years in the trenches. In the 1920s he worked as a mining engineer and bridge builder in the western American states and in China before settling in New York. A barroom discussion in 1934 with Leo Margulies, who was managing editor for Standard Magazines, prompted Scott to try writing fiction. He went on to create two of the most notable series characters in Western pulp magazines. In 1936, Standard Magazines launched, and in *Texas Rangers,* Scott under the house name of **Jackson Cole** created Jim Hatfield, Texas Ranger, a character whose popularity was so great with readers that this magazine featuring his adventures lasted until 1958. When others eventually began contributing Jim Hatfield stories,

Scott created another Texas Ranger hero, Walt Slade, better known as *El Halcón*, the Hawk, whose exploits were regularly featured in *Thrilling Western*. In the 1950s Scott moved quickly into writing book-length adventures about both Jim Hatfield and Walt Slade in long series of original paperback Westerns. At the same time, however, Scott was also doing some of his best work in hardcover Westerns published by Arcadia House; thoughtful, well-constructed stories, with engaging characters and authentic settings and situations. Among the best of these, surely, are *Silver City* (1953), *Longhorn Empire* (1954), *The Trail Builders* (1956), and *Blood on the Rio Grande* (1959). In these hardcover Westerns, many of which have never been reprinted, Scott proved himself highly capable of writing traditional Western stories with characters who have sufficient depth to change in the course of the narrative and with a degree of authenticity and historical accuracy absent from many of his series stories.

The employees of Thorndike Press hope you have enjoyed this Large Print book. All our Thorndike and Wheeler Large Print titles are designed for easy reading, and all our books are made to last. Other Thorndike Press Large Print books are available at your library, through selected bookstores, or directly from us.

For information about titles, please call:
    (800) 223-1244

or visit our Web site at:
    http://gale.cengage.com/thorndike

To share your comments, please write:
    Publisher
    Thorndike Press
    295 Kennedy Memorial Drive
    Waterville, ME 04901